North *of the* *Golden Gate*

MORE FIRESIDE TALES TO SHARE

MARGARET EDITH TRUSSELL

TALKING MOUNTAIN PUBLISHING
BODEGA BAY, CALIFORNIA 94923

[This book is printed on acid-free paper.]

ALSO BY MARGARET TRUSSELL:

Sierra Summers: Fireside Tales to Share with Young and Old.

For Ellie and Marian
For Dave, Bob, and John
For Bud, Dick, and Dottie

ACKNOWLEDGMENTS

I will not attempt to name the many people who have offered suggestions and encouragement, necessary ingredients to develop this book. But being a person given to turning to new tasks, I especially want to thank Linda Lewis Eshag, Catharine Flinn, Marie Nelligan, Gerry Olson, Irene Rust, Jill and Mary Sheppard and the members of my family for asking from time to time, "How is the book coming?" Without them there would be no book.

Julie at *Bits & PCs*, Jessie at *Business Services Unlimited*, and Mary at the Bodega Bay *Post Office*, have been helpful far beyond their obligations to a customer.

Armand Roth of *IBIS Information*, Theresa Silveira, and Alex Ling solved numerous computer challenges.

The cover was designed by Heidi at *ChromaGraphics*.

"The Reed Boat" first appeared in the *California Highway Patrolman*. "A Simple Cabin," in *Little Echoes*.

A number of the stories first saw light in English classes at Santa Rosa Junior College taught by Ida Egli, Peg Ellingson or Barbara McClure.

NORTH OF THE GOLDEN GATE
More Fireside Tales to Share

Published by:

Talking Mountain Publishing
Bodega Bay, California 94923-0621

© 1994 by Margaret Edith Trussell
First Printing 1994
Printed in the United States of America

Publisher's Cataloguing in Publication Data

Trussell, Margaret Edith, 1928-
        North of the Golden Gate: More Fireside Tales to Share

1.California Description and Travel.
2.California   Biography   3.Mountains-California.
4.American Wit and Humor.
5.American Short Stories. I. Title
Library of Congress Cat. Card No:93-60121
ISBN 0-9624235-2-1

CONTENTS

Preface vii

NONFICTION

The Morning Walk 11

A Walk from Ocean to Harbor 15

Abalone! Abalone? 34

The Reed Boat 43

Wheels! 53

Camp Thayer 61

A Simple Cabin 71

Footpaths 80

Adventuring in Youth Hostels 85

Those Mallard Ducks: The Human Perspective 98

FICTION

Those Mallard Ducks: The Avian Perspective 104

Conversations with Parker 112

A Fabulous Hike 124

Audited by the IRS 133

Cleaning the Garage 143

The Dumpster 154

Dusty MacBugTussle and the Human Genome 163

The House Sitters 173

Report from the Lake 185

The Big One! 192

ILLUSTRATIONS

Acknowledgements and thanks are due to the following for use of sketches, photographs, and maps reproduced in this book.

Dorothy Hill, photograph on page 45.

Barbara Ling, calligraphy on page 144.

Charles Nelson, map on page 17.

Margaret Quigley, photograph on the front cover and on page 49.

Bob Sorani, sketch on page 79.

Ella Trussell, photograph on page 123.

M.E. Trussell, photographs on pages 14, 63, 65, 82, 92, and 115.

Trussell family collection, photograph on page 41 and sketch on page 72.

Steve Underwood, photograph on the back cover.

Cynthia Van Kleeck, sketches on pages 58, 103, 111, 125, 134, 145, 155, 165, 176, 187, and 196.

"Listen! You can hear the corn grow..." Catharine Flinn, 1939.

PREFACE

North of the Golden Gate is a collection of tales, most of them set in coastal northern California, a sequel to my book, *Sierra Summers*. Like that book, it celebrates the simple pleasures.

The first section is nonfiction. Some of the narratives, such as "Abalone! Abalone?" "Camp Thayer," and "Those Mallard Ducks" are drawn from experiences growing up in the California of the 1930's and 1940's. It was a different era. The mailman brought "real" letters. Reading aloud was a popular way to share. All the members of the family sat down together at mealtime. Sunday was a day of rest. Most neighborhoods were safe, and children enjoyed a great deal of freedom.

Nowadays, though, it sometimes seems almost as if those years were in another world. Santa Rosa was a sleepy country center, population 13,000 in 1940; by contrast, there are over 113,000 in 1994.

People have changed, too. The Internal Revenue Service auditors, if not kinder, at least are gentler than the one in 1967 who was the inspiration for Mr. Twitchell in "Audited by the IRS." The same beneficent mellowing cannot be claimed for childhood.

The Senior Campers at "Camp Thayer" still were children even at the ripe old age of sixteen. Today's youngsters can't risk the luxury of leisurely maturation.

The voice of the children in "The House Sitters" isn't right for the nineties which the story purports to depict. I decided to include it, despite the anachronism, as a reminder of how much change has occurred.

There are, however, adventures that ring true today. Such nonfiction as "A Walk from Ocean to Harbor," "Footpaths," and "Adventuring in Youth Hostels," bridge the gap between past and present inviting the reader to share the "take only pictures; leave only footprints" lifestyle.

The nonfiction also sets the stage for much of the fiction as is most evident in "Those Mallard Ducks," a tale told twice, once from "The Human Perspective," and again from "The Avian Perspective." "Dusty MacBugTussle and the Human Genome" will seem familiar ground to anyone who has read "A Walk from Ocean to Harbor."

"A Fabulous Hike" is another example of the link between fiction and nonfiction. The events of a real hike are presented as fable, providing opportunity for a merry frolic with Plass-teek and Nile-on and even Diethylmetatoluamide (mosquito repellent).

Some of the fiction in *North of the Golden Gate*, such as "Cleaning the Garage," "The Dumpster," and "The Big One," is inspired by the "tall tale" tradition celebrated in our household by our Dad. His "now take another bite and I'll go on with the story" used familiar characters and events based upon experience.

Underlying the tales, and essential to them, is the oral tradition of our extended family, part of the bonding that links generations. When we were growing up, sometimes as many as thirty relatives came to our Santa Rosa home to share traditional dinners, turkey at Thanksgiving and leg of lamb at Easter. After the dessert, while the box of chocolates was going round the table, conversation would turn to arcane family lore, familiar accounts shared year after year.

All of our Great Grandparents had died before we children were born, but we knew them through the sharing. We knew the sophisticated English couple; she was merry, beautiful, and caring; he was a stern but loving father, a music critic for the *Yorkshire Post*. We knew the Minnesota pioneers who once lived in a sod house; she "had the disposition of an angel"; he was remembered as "cantankerous." We knew the forthright daughter of a Kentucky innkeeper, who said "If I had a name like 'Trussell,' I'd change it," and the pioneer named "Trussell" whom she married. We knew the plucky woman in Jefferson City, Missouri, who took in sewing to support her husband and three daughters after he, a U.S. Marshall, was disabled in the line of duty.

Culture is important; so is place. The names–Trussell, Rhodes, Brown, Scales—suggest Western Europe, but our forebears had sowed new lands. "Earth to earth, ashes to ashes, dust to dust..." affirms that all living things spring from Mother Earth, while "The hills of home..." reminds us that place is both universal and endlessly unique. The sense of place is a potent thread in the fabric of these tales.

Of course the dinner table conversation didn't stop with Great Grandparents but came around to

Grandparents, Great Aunts, Great Uncles, Aunts, Uncles, Parents, Cousins. And the children!

Children were the messengers, the connection between past and future. In the children were the last vestiges of the ancestral village, for they were the *only* ones who could look at everyone around that table and say, "Their blood flows in my veins." Just as we linked our people genetically, we united them culturally. Much had been sacrificed for us, and much was expected, as our Grandparents often pointed out.

It is only in retrospect that I recognize the pivotal position we children held. We were, indeed, the last generation of Americans before technological depersonalization: *Auto*mobiles, *Tele*vision, *Personal* computers, shopping centers, discount retail stores tore to pieces the circle of the extended family. We also were the last whose material "success" exceeded that of our parents.

This then, this family history, tells me who I am. It is the foundation for the stories.

The past has lessons for us. *Homo sapiens* is a gregarious species; sharing with one another is an important part of healthful living. We *must* be in charge of our lives, doers, not receivers. Perhaps the most important lesson is that small really is beautiful, and that it once was achieved not only in some distant place but here at home by people just like you and me.

M. E.. Trussell, Bodega Bay, 1994.

THE MORNING WALK

The sun is a hair-breadth line of liquid gold limning the eastern hills. A sheaf of golden arrows shoot toward blood-red puffs of cloud. A grand golden road spans the harbor. A fishing boat, its engine throbbing the shrill, strong sound of power, navigates the channel.

Linda and Theresa are standing at the trail junction. "Good morning! Good morning!"

We walk well-bundled toward the beach. Theresa leads; I bring up the rear. Every breath is a little cloud that hangs in front of its creator like a comic strip balloon. Frozen pinnacles, each tiny post capped by a miniature mesa, crumble under our feet, catapulting pebbles back to earth. The only sounds are a breeze in the grass and the crunch of sand underfoot.

We share the everyday fabric of our lives, the small happenings that seem so little yet mean so much. Theresa is taking a class at the junior college, learning American Sign Language, the speech of the deaf. She tells us it's a beautiful, an extraordinary language. She hopes someday to become an interpreter. Rick, her husband, is an expert at silk screen printing; he's working for a Petaluma t-shirt manufacturer.

Linda has been making beeswax candles, each one uniquely decorated with pressed flowers bonded into the wax. Tom and James, her husband and his crewman, are several hundred miles out fishing for albacore; they freeze the catch immediately after bringing them on board, so the boat may remain at sea for weeks before returning to port to discharge cargo.

Even in the depth of winter, green peeper frogs, welcome allies in my no-pesticide vegetable garden, proclaim their presence from sanctuaries in buckets and under boards. Birds, garter snakes, and legions of invertebrates arrive and depart year round according to their ancestral wisdom. All are engaged in a titanic struggle for the turf I brazenly call my own.

The sound of the surf swells as we climb the foredune. We cross a strange, warm breath of breeze. The rays of the low winter sun shine through a gap in the dunes lighting the crest of a breaking wave while its neighbors remain drab in the shadow. Bright, white spin-drift soars.

A river of fog pours down Salmon Creek valley connecting an inland ocean of cloud with a grim, grey bank to the west. The dark surrounds the sunny sanctuary of our beach.

The minus tide exposes a vast, firm, unbroken expanse, a clean slate on which we register our presence. We inhale the perfumed breath of the sea and heed the calls of birds, the crash of waves, and the susurrus wave washed sand. We walk three abreast watching for treasures.

"Here's a limpet shell! And another!" Linda hands them to Theresa. "Just right for your pine needle baskets."

"Wow! Do I have a prize for you, Linda." Theresa holds out a sea-tumbled sand-smoothed shard of bright blue bottle.

The fog-dark western sky is a fitting back-drop for an oriental painting. Thirteen egrets sail unhurried, bathed golden by the early light.

Theresa, our leader and our conscience, carries a large garbage sack and gathers styrofoam, plastic, and glass. Linda and I help save the world, the three of us bobbing up and down like Great Blue Herons fishing for frogs.

It's seven forty five, time to head for home. Restored by the mystical energy of a walk with friends, we are ready for the tasks of the day. Theresa leads the way back to the world of breakfast and the sounds produced by machines.

l-r Theresa and Linda carry a glass net float brought from Japan by ocean currents. Bumper supervises.

A WALK
FROM OCEAN TO HARBOR

INTRODUCTION. Sonoma Coast State Park, with headquarters at Salmon Creek, is 68 miles north of San Francisco. This narrative describes the Bodega Dunes area of the park.

The edge! The meeting place of land and sea, the two largest landforms on planet earth. No wonder even everyday events seem endowed with special significance, marvelous and unique.

The beach is a starting point for a visit to the edge. It may look like a desert, but actually it's a treasure house of nutrients that feed invertebrates numbering into the millions. And they, of course, become food for bigger critters on up the food chain.

"It looks vacant to me," says our guest. "There's nothing around but a few shore birds. Where are all those critters, and what's so great about the California coast?"

Well now, lots of the small critters live in holes or under flotsam; you'll see their hideouts when you walk across the beach. And such mammals as weasels, foxes, raccoons, and even deer come at night to feed; mostly all we see of them is their tracks. Some shore birds spend a lot of time here; other birds, such as hawks and vultures, come when the pickings are good.

As to the cause, upwelling water accounts for much of the riches. You see, the California current flows south along the coast. And the prevailing wind is from the northwest (which means it blows toward the southeast). When the wind blows across the current, warm surface water moves away from the land. Cold deep water rises to take its place, bringing nutrient materials from the depths within reach of surface plants and animals.

Upwelling water also is a cause of the coastal summer fog. When temperatures soar inland, air moves toward the interior drawing warm moist air over the cold water, and the coast has fog. Sometimes as little as four or five miles away, the sky is clear and the land is hot.

So welcome to the beach. Please respect park etiquette. Look but don't touch the plants and animals. And.....

NEVER, NEVER TURN YOUR BACK
ON THE OCEAN!

Nothing beats a map for determining where you are. The one on page 17 shows our walk from its place of beginning at South Salmon Creek Beach on the ocean (point A), through the dunes, to its end at Bodega Harbor (point B). Along the lower edge of the page below the map is a sketch which shows in side view the same walk along the line A--B.

PREVIEW.

This quick overview gives a feel for where we're

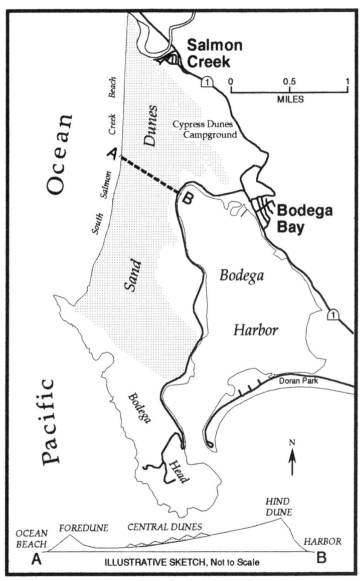

Figure 1. A Walk From Ocean to Harbor.

going. The ocean beach is dynamic, ever-changing. The sea itself is endlessly attractive; as Robert Frost put it, "The people along the sand....look at the sea all day." (*Neither Out Far nor In Deep*)

We leave the beach by climbing the foredune and descending into the central dunes. What a difference! The noise of the sea is muffled and the landscape clothed with vegetation.

The path rises gradually through the central dunes steepening as we near the crest of the hinddune, the highest point on our route. From that eminence we can see even the ocean breakers. The entire area from the beach (point A) to the crest of the hinddune (just before point B) is within the state park.

The steep slope from the crest to the harbor is shielded from the fiercest winds and is the domain of humankind. The land is privately owned. We take the path down to the waterfront, a gentler place than the ocean beach and often crowded with waterfowl, a birders' paradise. The walk ends at the water's edge at the harbor (point B).

The preview completed, let's return to the beach, which is our starting point.

OCEAN, BEACH, AND FOREDUNE

January 2.

Japanese glass floats come onto the beach after powerful storms and high tides. A woman finds one the size of a basketball. I find two small ones still in the wrappings that once attached them to the nets.

January 8.

Our friends look for sand dollars but find only one.   This beach in summer has lots more sand—and some more shells—than in winter, though Doran Beach (see map) is more sheltered and a better place to find shells.

February 21.

The tide is high and the sea rough. We are busy talking and hardly paying attention to the sea. Suddenly a huge deep green wave looms above us. We run as fast as we can, a hundred feet to higher ground. It snatches at our feet and ankles, but we escape. *NEVER TURN YOUR BACK ON THE OCEAN!*

March 12.

Surf Scoters swim nonchalantly among the breakers. These sturdy black ducks fish for clams by diving under the waves that break, taking advantage of the way the turbulent water ploughs the bottom.

May 4.

A driftwood Afghan Hound stands guard over a crenelated castle in the sand, the works of weekend beach sculptors.

June 11, 1981.

By-the-Wind-Sailors, *Velella velella,* small invertebrates related to sea anemones, have been washing up onto the beach by the millions for more than a month.   They are easy to recognize by their

transparent skeletons and sails and their beautiful blue
tentacles which rim the downward facing mouth. Ours
have sails angled to the right of the main axis of the
body, and prolonged southerly or westerly winds bring
them onto our beach. In years like this one when many
arrive, the odor of rotting *Velella* can permeate the air.

Birds with bluish bodies and rust colored breasts
skim back and forth just inches above the windrows of
fly-filled seaweed. Swallows, we think.

June 21. Scavengers.

Long-horned Beach Hoppers feed on seaweed
well above the high tide line. These inch-long
crustaceans have gray-brown bodies and orange
antennae. Like many other beach invertebrates, they
are nocturnal, which saves them from high
temperatures, drying winds, and diurnal predators.

Long-horned Beach Hoppers live in holes in the
sand near their food supply. They're excavation
experts, popping head first into their holes and kicking
sand out with their orange hind legs. Then they turn
head up and continue digging.

They are big enough to attract predators. Often
the tracks of shore birds or seagulls follow lines of their
holes.

June 25.

The nest with three inch-long, buff, speckled eggs
is high on the beach, well out of reach of the tide. Big
eggs, we think. According to *The Birder's Handbook*,
each one of a Sandpiper's eggs weighs about a fourth

as much as the mother! Shorebird babies need plentiful nutrition so as to be off as soon as they hatch.

The nest is a shallow depression in the sand, the eggs surrounded with small white chips that look like bits of seashell. They are so well camouflaged that I never can find the nest again.

July 31.

A Brown Pelican flies over the outermost breaker closely followed by a seagull. The pelican plops heavily into the water to scoop up some fish; the gull follows, anticipating a share of the catch.

August 19.

A huge dead Leatherback Sea Turtle, easily eight feet long, has been on our beach for several weeks. The *Press Democrat* has a picture of one recently netted near the Arctic Circle; it weighed 730 pounds. People speculate that such critters as these turtles are being lured to unaccustomed latitudes by the warm "el Niño."

August 20. High mist, low tide.

Thirteen egrets, their long necks tucked in, fly leisurely above the beach, brilliant white against a steel blue sky.

August 30.

Scattered clumps of Sea-Rocket with its fleshy stems and leaves and clusters of blue-pink flowers grow on the beach as much as a hundred yards in front of the foredune. Sometimes sandblasting destroys almost all the exposed stems and leaves, yet the plant grows back.

Sea-Rocket, Sea-Fig, Hottentot-Fig, and Sand-Verbena grow at the front of the foredune facing the sea. There are no trees. And Sea-Rocket, though an impressive survivor on the beach, does not grow elsewhere.

Not only do plants have to cope with wind, salt spray and sandblasting, but throughout the dunes the sand itself has little available nutrients and scant water holding capacity.

August 31, 7:00 p.m.

There is a bundle of black, heavy fish net near the high tide line; it must have been cast up this morning. The bird enmeshed in it is alive, trussed so tightly it can barely even move its head. It does not try to fight.

It is about the size of a bantam chicken, dark grey or black above with white on its breast and under its chin. There is a necklace-like line part way around its neck. It has a pointed bill. It may be a Lesser Grebe.

I use my knife to cut the net away. The worst injury seems to be where the strands have twisted tight against the flesh around the base of the right wing. When the victim finally is loose, the wing droops though it does not appear broken.

The bird stretches its neck, trying to defend itself. I pick it up and put it closer to the water. Twenty minutes later, it moves into the edge of the water, which seems to revive it. It begins to preen its injured wing.

Since then I keep a strong paper (not plastic) bag in my day pack. When I find another sick or injured bird, I'll be able to carry it to rescue people or to the harbor, where conditions for convalescing are gentler. [The entry for October 2 gives further information and precautions about rescuing birds.]

September 15. Scavengers.

Seagulls check out the fish of the day. They squabble over a dead crab but leave a live one alone. A medley of their footprints and cast-off bits of crab shell cover an area twenty feet in diameter.

There is an undulating scrape beside a line of tracks; some nocturnal animal—we think a Long-tailed Weasel—dragged a dead bird a hundred feet up the beach and into the foredune.

Other nocturnal mammals such as fox and raccoon, often venture as much as a hundred yards onto the open beach, where they hunt among the flotsam.

They are the night shift at the beach; people are the day shift. The two rarely meet.

September 21.

The sand around a partly buried piece of seaweed is disturbed and full of holes. The invertebrates that build these burrows are safely underground during the day.

Small black flies rise in droves as we walk across

the beach. Such populations soar and crash. At various times the fresh seaweed may swarm with bugs, flies, and/or small beach hoppers (a different species from Long-horned Beach Hoppers).

September 25, Trash.
Balloons, a dozen of them in orange, white, blue, and red are newly washed onto the beach. One says "Happy Birthday." We continue to find others on the beach for two months. Perhaps the people who launch these don't realize that an animal that eats one won't have a "happy day"?

October 1.
More tracks! A skunk leaves a long line of footprints in front of the foredune. It makes a brief detour into the beach grass and back, perhaps to catch a mouse. Dimpled pathways made by mice sometimes are as much as four inches wide. They occur throughout the dunes.

October 2, 8:00 a.m.
A small black and white bird with feathers in disarray huddles on the sand. We think it is a Common Murre.
What to do? There's nobody else around to help. I take a large paper bag out of my daypack and gently move the unresisting bird into it. We are careful to leave the top of the bag open so the bird will have plenty of air.
As soon as we get to a phone we try to find

someone to care for it. Time after time we reach only answering machines; finally the switchboard operator at the Sheriff's Office suggests the Wildlife Center.

Pete at The Wildlife Center in Kenwood, (707) 575-1000 (phone answered 24 hours a day) arranges for us to take it to their veterinarian (no cost to us). He also cautions us not to set the bird on anything hard, such as a floor, because its keel easily can be injured. (We carry it in its paper bag on the car seat.)

He advises us not to try to give it water; it likely will have to be force-fed, which is not a task for amateurs. And finally he says to be sure that the bird gets plenty of air.

We found the bird at 8 a.m. and got it to the veterinarian at 10:05. The Wildlife Center later told us that it was a Rhinoceros Auklet, a bird that is unusual this near to shore. It was too sick to be saved, so center personnel gave it to the ornithologist at Sonoma State University who would use it in his teaching.

Pete said our paper bag was OK, but an even better way to carry an injured bird is to approach it from behind and put a towel over it. Be sure to check that its head is not bent back. Wrap it gently and when possible put it into a padded box with air holes.

Pete also told us not to try to handle big predatory birds. Even a sick one is very powerful and dangerous to anyone getting too close. If in doubt, phone the Wildlife Center.

October 10, Beachcombing.

This morning I find a sand dollar about the size

of my thumbnail, also the shells of three limpets, a scallop, and a mussel. This shore is exposed to the open ocean, so many shells break up without ever coming onto the beach.

There are, however, a wide variety of "treasures" for beachcombers. Some past finds:

A legal size abalone with a holdfast of bull whip kelp attached to its shell.

One—never two—of a pair of things: oars, swim fins, shoes,

A diver's wristwatch still telling the correct time.

Cans of soft drinks, still unopened

November 2.

This morning there was a small private airplane on the beach. The pilot made an emergency landing on the wet sand yesterday after a problem developed in the fuel line. The repairs were simple, and she flew it off this afternoon.

November 12.

A dancing line of 40 Sanderlings feeds at the edge of each wave up and down the wet beach, probing in the sand or grabbing an occasional morsel carried by the water. These little shorebirds are international travellers. They spend summers at Arctic Canadian and Greenland nesting grounds and winters on the sandy beaches of every continent.

December 20.

Deep heel-and-toe prints of two joggers and the

four-toed-with-toenails prints of their dog run up the beach before we get there. My own shallow, even prints are typical of walkers.

People and their "baggage" are ubiquitous. The beach can support heavy recreational use but the dunes are fragile. ORVs operating illegally in the dunes leave wide swaths of crushed vegetation and loose sand. Horse and rider create deeply entrenched paths. Feral cats take a heavy toll of birds.

THE CENTRAL DUNES

The central dunes is the area between the foredune, which faces the ocean, and the hinddune, which faces the harbor. These central dunes are oriented transverse to the shore rather than parallel to it.

Whoops! *What* "central dunes"? Large areas are almost featureless.

History suggests what happened. Years ago livestock pastured here damaged plant cover and accelerated erosion. Later people planted the dunes to reduce the amount of sand blowing into the harbor.

Dunes constantly are built and rebuilt. Consider a grain of sand. The wind rolls and carries it across the beach and up the foredune, down the foredune, through the central dunes, up the hinddune, and into the harbor. But European Beach Grass retains more sand in the foredune than the native grasses did; the grains in the central dunes move on up the hinddune but are not replaced. Large flat "deflation" areas result.

On a stormy day wind, spray, sandblasting, and noise diminish dramatically as we go from the windward to the leeward side of the foredune. It's easy to understand why so few species of plants live on the foredune whereas many live in the central dunes behind it.

Beach grass, Sea Fig and Hottentot Fig are abundant, and there are such hardy perennials as Yellow Bush Lupine, coyote bush, and monkey flower. There is one tree, the Monterey Cypress.

A hard freeze several years ago killed large patches of Hottentot Fig. In some of the deflation areas, ground-hugging plants such as Deerweed and Beach-Primrose send out tendrils in starlike patterns as they colonize the blackened mulch.

The mammals that venture onto the beach have their homes here in the central dunes. Birds are different, though. Except for such scavengers and predators as vultures, crows, and hawks, most of the central dunes birds rarely go to the beach.

The path through the central dunes rises gradually as we walk toward the harbor. We feel, more than we see, that we are going uphill.

April 22.

A dove sits on a flimsy nest made of a few pieces of straw on a Monterey Cypress branch five feet off the ground and a yard from the path. I observe her (or him, as the case may be, for both parents share the care of the young) from the corners of my eyes every morning. She is as still as a porcelain dove; only her bright eye reveals that she is alive.

Her body screens the squabs until one day beside her there is one almost as big as she is. It is all pinfeathers and fuzz on May 17. Two days later the nest is empty.

June 6, 1990.

There is an inch-long bone, white from weathering, on a small ridge in the central dunes. Two bird bands, one aluminum with writing on it and the other ivory colored plastic, ring the bone. I take it to the ornithologist at the Marine Lab.

He phones several days later. The bird was a Sanderling that Marine Lab personnel had banded as an adult on September 4, 1980. People sighted it again during August to November 1981 and possibly in August, 1982, eight years ago, after which it was not reported.

Sanderlings are shorebirds and ordinarily would not be in the central dunes. Probably a small hawk caught it at the beach and carried it to this high place to eat.

June 11.

An adult quail flies away as we come. A fluffy, spotted baby, so close we could touch it, remains in place, motionless except that it moves its head. Camouflage can be the best protection.

June 20.

This morning when I return from the beach

after being there less than an hour, there are tracks of
two quail overlapping my earlier footprints. Paths serve
many creatures.

November 5.

There are two ticks crawling on my pantleg after
our morning walk. I use a comb to lift them off and
immerse them in a dish of water to which I've added a
few drops of detergent.

We don't see any ticks during the summer,
despite going for a walk every day. In this area tick
season for us starts after the first rains in the fall,
though some places have it all summer.

December 5.

A tiny bubbly stream of water is trickling down
the trunk of the Monterey Cypress near the path. The
dark green, thick foliage sieves moisture from the fog
or rain. So consistent is the supply that a light green
algae grows on the lower trunk of this tree.

This fine cypress is vigorous and sturdy though
bent by the northwest wind. Its shallow roots spread
widely, gathering nutrients and water from a large area.
In fact several of them cross the path, forming wooden
ridges now quite worn.

We've climbed the gentle slope through the
central dunes and up the hinddune. Now we've
reached the highest point, well above the top of the
foredune. We can see the ocean again; the sounds of
the sea are louder and there's more bite to the wind.

HINDDUNE, HARBOR AND BAY.

May 3.

It's evening, and the sky is almost dark when we reach the crest. A Great Horned Owl stands atop a post only twenty feet away, observing unblinking with huge bright eyes. Power! Its formidable beak and white moustache, its mighty talons, its impressive size, all underscore that this is not a friendly encounter and that the earth belongs not only to people. Leisurely, it spreads its wings and disappears silently into the darkness.

As soon as we cross the crest and start down the leeward side toward the harbor the sound and the wind lessen. Here in this gentler place *Homo sapiens* has put down roots, roads, homes, fences, wires, poles, garbage cans, gardens and automobiles. The species also has modified the land by bringing in improved soil for gardens and introducing domesticated plants.

Many more species of plants grow here than in the central dunes. More trees, too. In addition to the cypress, there are willow, eucalyptus, and several species of pine.

There are as well a great many other animals, both domesticated and wild. And the harbor and its environs are particularly interesting because of the large numbers and numerous species of birds that come here, including migratory waterfowl.

March 1.

Birdwatchers! A line of cars is parked beside the

rail ponds. A clutch of people with eyes glued to their binoculars walk along the paths to either side exclaiming in hushed tones from time to time and paying scant attention to where they are going.

May 6.

An osprey circles the harbor, then hovers, quivering white. Suddenly it plunges into the water and comes up with a fish in its talons. It maneuvers the fish into a head first, more streamlined, position and flies away.

June 21.

My neighbor puts out food for the raccoons every evening. She invites our English guests and me to come and see them. The first one arrives about dark, followed by four others. One big fellow sits up to eat, looking for all the world like a huge chipmunk. The rest seem less secure and remain on all fours.

October 1.

Thud! A small bird with a yellow cap, a Golden Crowned Kinglet, lies on the doormat. Its legs and feet are intertwined; it quivers; it appears to be dying.

What to do? Don't panic, remember: an injured animal needs rest and warmth. I place it in my cupped hand against my shoulder under my sweater. It moves slightly but settles down and does not try to escape. Ten minutes later, it begins to move purposefully. I put it atop a fence post; it hesitates a moment then flies to the top of a cypress tree.

EPITOME

This morning we stand on the crest of the foredune. Beyond the breakers, whitecaps look like distant fishing boats, but no prudent small boat skipper would be out on a day like this. Six seagulls fly chasing a seventh that has a fish in its mouth, wheeling, dodging, feinting, like kids playing sandlot football.

The sand is wet beneath the cypress trees in the central dunes. And scattered droplets show that even the beach grass has strained water from early fog.

Mouse tracks, mouse paths, mouse boulevards criss-cross our trail, signifying a mouse population explosion. Mouse predators will be dining well.

At the crest of the hinddune we turn for one last look at the ocean. Then we start down the road toward the harbor and the bay beyond.

A Brown Pelican plunges into the harbor fishing for its breakfast. Seven White Pelicans in a circle swim toward each other in the shallow water dipping and raising their bills as they close ranks on the fish.

The edge is a world of its own. Look; take notes; ask yourself questions.

Explore! Enjoy!

ABALONE! ABALONE?

It must have been in 1939 that Pop first took Ellie and me abaloneing. We'd been clamoring to go. Finally one morning he said, "There's a good minus tide this afternoon, girls. Let's go abaloneing." We ran to get our jackets, hug our Mother, who was staying home with the baby, and jump into the car before Pop could change his mind.

It was a sunny, clear day at the coast; we could see for miles. The superstructure of a ship moved along the horizon. Pop explained that the earth's curvature concealed the hull from our view. Inland there was dark green coniferous forest, and nearby grassy hills shimmered in the sunlight. The road followed the gently sloping surface of a coastal terrace which ended off to our left in a bluff that plunged to a narrow beach.

From time to time we'd see little rocky islands which rose out of the blue and white water. Pop called them sea stacks. He said that the land once extended farther into the sea; these islands were all that remained, the rest having been eroded away.

North of Russian Gulch the car wound up a long hill till we reached a turnoff where we could park. Pop said, "We'll put rocks behind the wheels so the car won't roll."

We looked down the steep slope to the distant cove that was our goal. (Pop always maintains that there are more fish and less competition at hard-to-reach spots.)

All three of us were wearing blue jeans, long-sleeved sweatshirts, warm socks and sturdy shoes. Pop had on his oldest clothes and carried another outfit so he could change when he got out of the water.

Rock picking didn't require much gear. Pop used a bar made of an old automobile spring to pry the abalones off and a gunny sack to carry them. Ellie and I were prepared too, with big hunting knives in sheaths on our belts—essential, we thought, to any outing.

Most of the beach was boulders ranging in size from a steamer trunk to a four bedroom house. These were overgrown with seaweed. Some of them rested on bedrock, while a gravelly floor underlay others. There was an area of coarse gravel liberally mixed with pieces of shell over to one side. Chunks of driftwood and masses of seaweed were lodged above the high tide line. And everywhere was the wonderful fragrance of ocean, hard to describe but never to be forgotten once we'd savored it.

It had been evident from the very first that Pop was taking us for an outing, while *he* got the abalone. He reminded us of the rules when we reached the beach where the outgoing tide already revealed species usually hidden from view. "Now stay out of the water, both of you," he commanded in his most authoritarian voice and with his strict school teacher frown. "Don't even get your feet wet, or there'll be war!"

Ellie and I, ages 9 and 11, knew our father meant business when we heard that no-nonsense tone in his voice.   So we watched obediently while he inched into the icy water first knee-deep, then hip-deep, then up to his shoulders, all the while feeling under ledges and in niches, wherever his fisherman's sixth sense told him there might be an abalone.

We had great confidence in his ability to cope with any situation, so it never occurred to either of us to worry as he gradually receded deeper and deeper. And when he finally disappeared behind a boulder, we soon lost interest in looking for him and turned to our own devices.

We watched sea anemones sweep their colorful tentacles to grasp bits of shell that we dropped on them.   Small fish in the tidepools darted in and out, hiding in the seaweed.   Hermit crabs scuttled into crevices.   There were starfish, and Ellie found a many rayed sunflower star that we carried around for a few minutes before letting it go again.   We collected shells and sea-tumbled-smooth colored pebbles.   In fact, we enjoyed ourselves immensely, all the while keeping our feet out of the water, for we were experienced enough to know that if we managed to stay dry, our chances of coming again would rise exponentially.

We'd really hardly gotten into the swing of exploration   when   Ellie   pointed   at   a   curious protuberance on the recurved lower edge of a huge wall-like grey boulder and said in a tentative voice, "Isn't that an abalone?"

We both drew our hunting knives. Neither of us

remembers who pried off the first abalone, but by the time our soaking wet, shivering parent returned with his catch, each of us had limits of our own. (Nowadays it is not legal to use a knife as a pry bar in taking abalone.) "And we didn't even get our feet wet, Pop," Ellie told him.

Of course, we were rather small to carry such heavy loads the half mile up the bluff to the road. So Pop sorted the abalone into two gunny sacks. First he hauled one load up the path for a hundred yards or so. Then he went back to get the other. Up and back, up and back, we made our way to the car.

With such success on our initial hunt, we naturally wanted to go next time. Pop included us and sometimes our friends as well on nearly every such expedition for years. He did, however, somewhat change the rules. After that first experience, people were responsible to carry their own catches from the beach to the car. It was awhile, too, before he again took us to the cove below his "inaccessible bluff."

Abalone outings developed a sort of rhythm. We'd leave home the preceding evening if the minus tide was going to be in the morning, drive from Santa Rosa to the coast and camp out so as to get an early start. Often we'd stop somewhere enroute to eat dinner. Then we'd stay at Russian Gulch or at Fort Ross, sleeping on the ground and waking before daybreak to meet the tide.

There were some amusing sidelights to these expeditions. Once when Ellie and I were in our early teens, Pop invited one of his fellow high school teachers to come with us. We four stopped to eat dinner at a Russian River resort. After we finished our meal, the waiter brought each of these middle aged men a check for two people. When we got back to the car, Pop's friend laughed, "Dusty, which one is your girlfriend and which one is mine?"

Good minus tides always seemed to occur very early on cold mornings. Pop pointed out it was best to be there ready to go into the water about an hour before low tide. His "Time to get up, girls," would rouse us while stars were still in the night sky. Having slept in most of our clothes, we hastily donned shoes and jackets, shook the dew off our sleeping bags and bundled the bedding into the car. Meanwhile, he had kindled a campfire and cooked hotcakes, which we bolted before departing for the shore.

Nobody had wet suits; abaloneing always was a bone-chilling activity. The first person out of the water selected a sheltered spot and built a fire. As the rest of us emerged, we'd congregate around it drinking coffee and turning first our faces then our backs toward the warmth. When finally we steamed like teakettles and our hands stopped shaking from the cold, one by one we'd stand behind a rock to change into dry jeans and sweatshirts. And afterward, until washday, that wonderful smoky fragrance of burning driftwood lingered over us whenever we wore our rough clothes.

Pop had an extra responsibility. When he got out of the water, he'd pry a couple of abalone from their shells, clean them and slice the firm white meat.

Someone would start bacon frying in a big skillet.

Pop would place the slices atop a boulder and pound them with his pry bar till they were exactly the right consistency. Then he'd drop them into the pan with the sizzling bacon grease, fry them a few moments, turn them briefly, and brunch was ready. There is no better way to eat abalone. (Preparing abalone on the beach is no longer legal because of the likelihood that some fishermen would use the practice to conceal undersized or over-limit catches.)

When everyone was warm and well fed, we'd extinguish the fire and head for home. There we'd hang the damp bedding on the line to dry, clean and pound the abalone, and consult the tide book to plan our next expedition.

Of course, each trip provided its own adventures. Once at Fort Ross we caught an octopus. It measured 10 feet from the tip of one tentacle to the tip of another (which isn't very big as octopi go). Ellie and I, still in the Hunter Stage of our personal cultural evolution, killed it and brought it ashore.

Pop, who will sample anything reported to be edible, pounded a piece and fried it. We all watched as he put the sandwich into his mouth and bit down hard to take a man-size bite. *Tried* to take a bite, that is; though the bread separated, the octopus stayed in one piece. "It's good flavored, but a bit tough to chew," he observed.

Another time Pop rigged a bamboo pole and taught us to fish in little pools under boulders. He was the only successful poke pole angler and brought in an eel-like grey green fish. He also was the only one to eat it—the rest of us balked at the strange color and reptilian form though, as I remember, it turned white in cooking, and he claimed it was delicious.

One of the joys of growing up in the thirties and forties was such expeditions to the coast. When we were older, we often included college friends. Some of these people still lovingly speak of good times they had on what was their sole experience with the hunting and gathering mystique.

By the 50's and 60's, abalone became more and more difficult for rock pickers to find. Ellie tried skindiving for them in 1975, but she said floating on the surface and looking at the bottom through waving kelp made her seasick. Once was enough.

For awhile it seemed as if those days were gone for good. Say goodbye to the camaraderie. Goodbye to the primordial fragrance of seaweed, salt water, and burning driftwood. We even missed the corrosive mixture of sand and sea which lodged inside wet clothing and scrubbed our skins to a rosy red.

We went clamming but soon tired of clams. We pried mussels off surf-sprayed boulders, but most of us didn't like to eat mussels. Then there's red tape; both clams and mussels periodically are affected with the deadly "red tide," so any expedition to gather them has to start with a call to the County Health Department to be sure they're clear.

In retrospect, we just hadn't been paying attention to what really drew us to the shore. We finally realized that it's lots more fun to *observe* the

We found we'd rather see than eat them.

plants and animals than to kill them. And our friends
enjoy it, too. Tidepooling set us free. It absolved us
ofthe responsibility to catch, kill, clean, cook, and
consume.

Abaloneing was great, and those days are still
fresh in family folklore. But now when we think of
seaweed, salt water, and burning driftwood, we don't
regret that we can't get abalone. We invite some
friends, bring a picnic lunch and a nature guide and
head for the bay mudflats or for a rocky beach at the
next good minus tide!

THE REED BOAT

"Ahoy there! Where are you going in that craft?" the Coast Guard station hailed us as we glided sinuously, silently across the harbor on "Hoorah," impelled by the currents and the breeze. The voice, bull-horn thunderous, disembodied, tried to sound authoritative. But it choked a little on "craft" as if it had started to pronounce something else then panicked at the final instant. It succeeded only in sounding surprised, almost incredulous, as if the speaker didn't believe, perhaps didn't want to believe, what he saw.

Now this is the story of the last voyage of the Hoorah, an ecologically non-polluting, biodegradable, recyclable boat. But it has its beginnings in the moist earth and warm climate of the Sacramento Valley, where the reeds grow luxuriantly, tall and strong, and people dream dreams of adventure and bygone times and faraway places.

We geographers—six students and I—had been talking about Thor Heyerdahl's book, *The Ra Expeditions*, the account of his amazing voyage across the Atlantic in a reed boat. Geographers are adventurous folk. So when someone said, "Reeds grow in the Sacramento Valley. We could build a reed boat," someone else said "Let's." And we did.

Well, it wasn't quite that simple. We

immediately encountered skeptical colleagues and friends: "I wonder if sharks eat vegetables?" and "That grass will go straight to the bottom; only Egyptian papyrus will float." Such critics clearly were ignorant of the fact that the California Indians used to navigate San Francisco Bay and its tributaries in boats built of reeds ancestral to those we proposed to use. First we must lay fears to rest. We'd test the building materials.

We experimented by floating two-inch sections of dried reed in dishes of water. They stayed high and dry for a full week. Even after they began to rot and smell like the discard bin at the produce market they remained very buoyant and would provide ample flotation. We threw them away and declared the experiment a success.

The reeds occupy low-lying adobe soil once part of a vast tule marsh that was regularly inundated by overflow from the Sacramento River and its tributaries. The marsh was a major resource for wildlife including a stopping place for migratory waterfowl.

Most of the marsh now has been drained and planted to domesticated crops, largely rice. Some land, such as ditches and overflow channels, continues to support reeds. These, together with wildfowl refuges and gun club holdings, remain as vestiges of the huge former marshes.

The reeds, which grow as much as ten feet tall in favorable sites, are cylindrical. The largest are more than an inch in diameter at the base. They have tough, dark green outer skins. The pulpy centers consist of millions of tiny closed air-filled cells

Reeds grow in the Sacramento Valley

separated by parchment-like membranes. They are very buoyant.

We got our reeds toward the end of September. But reading, experimentation and observation convince us that the optimum time to cut them is late summer when they are mature but still vigorous.

Reeds need to be cut green, then sun dried for four or five days before being lashed into bundles. They shrink as they dry. If uncured ones are used, the lashings soon will loosen, and the boat will fall to pieces. Dark green, mature reeds are best, tough, flexible and durable. If they have little spots of dry rot, they are too old and soon will deteriorate. If they are too young, the outer skin is not tough enough, and they will shrink excessively as they dry.

Reeds taller than a man flourish along swampy low spots in the Sacramento Valley. A rancher was glad to allow us to cut all we wanted. (Farmers consider them a nuisance, because they choke drainage ditches and crowd out pasture grasses. Nevertheless, they are important habitat which supports a wide variety of animals.)

Hoorah's first career was as a "racing reed," which is about as different from a "racing shell" as water is from air. The story of those events will keep for another day. Suffice it to say that as soon as we Geographers began planning Hoorah, we challenged two other departments of the University to construct reed boats.

The three departments held a great regatta a month later. A hundred spectators, including local historians, university rooters, and a reporter from the Chico TV station watched Hoorah speed first across the finish line. Many had never seen a reed boat before. Probably none had seen one in use.

But I'm getting ahead of my story. Once we had found a supply of building materials, design was the next task. Essentially the boat is constructed of small bundles of reeds tied together at the bases and then overlapped and lashed into long continuous bundles, much as thread is formed by arranging short fibers of wool or cotton. Heyerdahl's book included photographs of a number of such vessels still used in various parts of the world.

But we wanted an American style, so we sent a scout to the state Indian Museum in Sacramento to examine the one that was there. Considerable creative imagination went into the construction of Hoorah as well. She was indeed "All American."

The boat was sixteen feet long and five and one-half feet maximum width. She had an upturned bow. The raw materials consisted of three pickup loads of reeds, a ball of binder twine and a ball of tree rope. The rope and the twine cost twenty dollars.

When we took Hoorah out of the water after her maiden voyage, we discovered one of the shortcomings of such boats. Even though the reeds may not have soaked up any water, every one of them is covered with a thin film of it. When dry, the boat was light and easy to carry. When wet, it was surprisingly heavy. Perhaps we should have built her smaller for that reason.

At the time we didn't realize that it was

important to store the boat in a dry place with good air circulation. As she got older, the interior reeds began to rot and to take up moisture very quickly. Hoorah was stored outdoors; rain hastened the decomposition. And while she still floated well on short voyages (the only kind we ever took), she was water-soaked afterward and aged rapidly.

Hoorah made two last voyages after the great regatta. The first was a visit to the lake at Santa Rosa City Park. An elementary school class of nine-year-olds took turns riding on this craft "like those the Native Americans used to build." It was thrilling. Every child was a proper "Indian" and helped navigate. And when they took Hoorah out, she walked to the trailer easily on four dozen little feet—childpower.

But her final and most memorable voyage was at Bodega Bay, with its sheltered harbor on the coast north of San Francisco. She was showing her age; some of the reeds were becoming frayed, and mildew had invaded her interior. Clearly her days were numbered. It seemed fitting that the final voyage would be across salt water not far from San Francisco Bay, where the aboriginal boats that had inspired her creation had navigated a century ago.

No possible preparation for a luxurious cruise was overlooked. We mounted a kayak mast and sail on the bow. We jammed long boards between the reeds for centerboards. Each of us had a steering paddle.

Actually, Hoorah was not water-tight at all but a raft held up by the buoyancy of each of the individual reeds. It was flexible, sinuous and yielding, soft to sit

l-r Ellie and Sherry preparing the boat for the final voyage, across the harbor at Bodega Bay.

on but difficult to walk on. We put boards across to stiffen the deck so we wouldn't need to step in the water.

Only three who came that day were mariners. The others obstinately refused to set foot aboard and, indeed, scoffed at our chances of crossing a mile and a half of water without mishap. The crew embarked joyfully, undaunted by gloomy predictions. As soon as we were a few hundred feet out from the dock, curious boatmen circled us, inquiring as to our destination and asking if we needed a tow. One lady asked, "What is that, a haystack?" She was not trying to be funny, though for some reason our landlubber friends on shore doubled over with laughter.

We barely had embarked when we began to appreciate what a treat this voyage would be. We were dry. The sun was warm on our backs. Hoorah glided quietly along. A saucy seagull cheered our progress.

We decided to return to the dock to share this rare opportunity with our friends. Their jesting, surely, would turn to appreciation, and they'd want to ride too when they saw how delightful a voyage could be. So we paddled mightily and pivoted the boat around, re-set the sail—and nothing happened.

Hoorah continued her unbroken progress toward the opposite shore. The combination of wind and current had us in their grip, and there was no return. Experimentation showed that we could steer, provided we continued in the general direction determined by natural forces. But the ride was effortless and peaceful, much like the sensation of floating in a balloon. The boat embraced the waves, curving its form to fit them. We were *of* the water, not *on* it.

We looked down at pastures of waving eelgrass grazed by creatures of the deep. We imagined monsters, huge and terrifying, but they seemed improbable on such a lovely day. Unlike the boatmen, who continued to inspect us with wonder or with amusement, the birds seemed less affected by our passage than by the noisy Twentieth Century craft. We saw a cormorant, its long profile low in the water like a surfaced submarine, its rapier beak poised for fish. It viewed us unconcernedly then returned its attention to dinner. We thought reed craft and seabirds natural friends. We staunchly assured one another that Hoorah was very seaworthy and undoubtedly could get to the Farallone Islands, if only we could steer.

While we navigated the harbor in the curious craft, our five landlubber friends circumnavigated it in a car. By the time we had passed the Coast Guard station, having allayed their official fears by assuring them that we were not going to venture out to sea, our friends were awaiting us at the launching ramp. A sizeable crowd had joined them. One would think people'd never seen a reed boat before!

Fortunately, there always seems to be a crowd where there's a reed boat. And a forest of hands lifted the craft out of the water and set it on the trailer. That's the way it was when we left Bodega Bay.

Hoorah clearly was past her prime. So one day we pulled the lashing ropes off, broke up the bundles, and gently let the tired hull return to the soil. It seemed a fitting end for a reed boat.

It must be time to cut reeds again. I've been thinking about the Hoorah all day long.

WHEELS!

In the 1930's and 40's there were several vehicles in the barnyard at Aggie's Ranch. One was her transportation that she drove to and from work. Another was an ancient flatbed truck. When one wheel was jacked up, it powered a circular saw by means of a belt running between the rim and the saw axle. Mr. Lawrey used this equipment when he cut firewood for sale as his contribution to keeping the ranch and its people afloat in the sea of adversity that buffeted so many during the Depression.

And there was Aggie's once-snappy 1928 Chevrolet coupe, originally an extravagant wedding gift from her then-wealthy husband; now, with flat tires, sagging doors and weatherbeaten paint, only a roost for the barnyard birds. To adult observers, it was ready for the junk yard; to us teenagers it could be handsome again with just a little work.

It was probably because I was 16 and old enough to have a driver's license that Aggie in one of her typically impulsive acts of generosity gave me the car. If Ellie had been of age, she no doubt would have been, at the very least, half owner.

Aggie's loving, if unforesightful, gifts to us children often cost our parents a heavy toll, and this one was no exception. "Can't have it" was too strong a statement, even from our stern father. "It will take a lot of repairs" was inadequate to discourage an avid first-owner. The threat that "If it doesn't work out, it goes to the junk yard," precluded complacency.

So we patched the tires and pumped them up, and Pop towed it home. If he muttered, his oaths were inaudible. Perhaps he knew what unlimited opportunities that vehicle offered to banish teenage boredom. Over the years, it presented us with a never-ending series of crises, minor to major. The first was, could it be saved?

It was touch and go. Fortunately Pop was an excellent and generous mechanic. For days he came home from work to throw off his coat and tie, don greasy overalls and perform arcane rites beneath the hood. Finally the "simple" four cylinder engine belched blue smoke and sputtered with the promise of returning life.

My only attempts at mechanical repairs went down to defeat. Like the day I took the carburetor apart to check the gas line as I'd watched Pop do. Despite my tinkering, the engine wouldn't start. Finally he came to the rescue. Though the initial problem proved to have been an empty gas tank, the car wouldn't run till he back-tracked my repair efforts and turned the carburetor float right side up.

One lesson we learned early and well. "Never," said Pop, "Never hold the crank with thumb on one side and fingers on the other. You easily could break your thumb if the crank kicks back when the engine starts."

We always were careful to hold it correctly, and when the crank flew up, it simply jerked out of our hands. We had, as it proved, plenty of opportunity to practice.

Some tasks were grist for our mill. Ellie and I soon were proficient patchers of those rotten rubber innertubes. We'd pry the tire off the rim, find the leak, repair it, and re-assemble the wheel. We became so skilled, that we could have qualified as pit crew for the Indy 500.

By the end of the first week, the engine would run, albeit reluctantly. And the tires would stay up for at least a day at a time. But there were more serious obstacles to be overcome before the car could be licensed to be driven on the public highways and byways—mainly byways, our parents fervently hoped. The roof leaked. The upholstery was in rags, and more serious still, the wooden door posts were riddled with dry rot. No wonder the doors sagged!

I bought coated canvas to repair the roof—no metal tops in those days—and splurged my savings on blue denim to re-upholster the interior. Good ol' Pop donned coveralls and replaced the door posts. And to gild the lily, I painted the body school-bus orange and the fenders, running boards, and top black.

I thought a nice name would be "Daffodil." Pop, with characteristic foresight, dubbed it "The Golden Menace," and nobody but me ever called it anything else.

Preparations were over when we'd patched to the operational level; the next challenge was actually to put the car into service. The big day finally arrived, the day to attach the license, the day of joy at driving down the street.

There was a crowd of teenagers for the inaugural journey. Unlike some coupes which had rumble seats, the Golden Menace had a trunk, which proved to be quite an asset. When we wanted more space, we removed the lid, enabling us to fit three or four passengers in the back, an unusually commodious accommodation.

I drove carefully if somewhat erratically, getting used to the temperament of wheels of my very own. We tootled around town—the car was still too delicate a mechanism to be risked over long distances. That first trip converted us instantly into motorists. Perhaps it was symptomatic that a day or so later Pop tried to persuade me that the speed limit on the city streets was 20 miles per hour.

In addition to its contribution to teenage mobility and to the sheer joy of driving, the Golden Menace was a powerful educational force in those days before the advent of driver education classes in schools. Ellie reminded me just the other day of the first time she ever drove. She took over the wheel when we were well beyond the city limits and headed out Sonoma Avenue which at that time was a quiet road with walnut orchards on both sides. All went well till we got to Summerfield Road where, she says, she "hadn't gotten the concept of turning yet and almost ran it into the ditch" when she tried to go around the corner.

Once the Golden Menace was licensed, keeping

it in working order was my responsibility, though generous relatives added an occasional boost. The time was just at the end of World War II. It was no problem to get gas ration coupons, but new tires or battery were impossible to find.

Occasionally on a really good day when everything went well and if spark and throttle levers were set exactly right, the battery had enough oomph to start the car. The rest of the time we cranked, which wasn't all that bad, especially for the licensed drivers, who usually sat behind the wheel while their juniors stood out front and labored. My sister still bears a mental scar from the day the engine died at the intersection of Fourth and Mendocino, and she had to climb out and crank. She grins but not too sincerely, as she explains from between clenched teeth that Santa Rosa's entire population of 12,605 walked by before she got it going.

Morning starts were the hardest of all. We'd crank and crank, re-set the spark and throttle levers and crank again, trade off and crank again. Our Uncle Harry, a travelling salesman for Exide Automotive Batteries, solved the problem. We garaged the Golden Menace at our Grandmother's home, where he stored

Alas! We searched attic, closet, and garage, turned out dusty boxes, badgered our kinfolk into exploring their ancient treasures, offered rewards. Everybody's sure there is one, but Nobody came up with a photo of the Golden Menace. Finally Cindy Van Kleeck obliged with her mental image of the little car (page 58)

The entire population of Santa Rosa, 12,605 people, walked by the intersection of Fourth and Mendocino Streets before Ellie could get the Golden Menace started again.

some of his stock, and he helped us rig a cable to
jump-start off one of his heavy duty truck batteries.
Then the engine would warm up while we drove to
school, and that poor, ancient battery would charge a
little. Cranking would be easier for the rest of the day.
We experienced many adventures in the little car.
Once I drove it at the speed limit, fifty five miles an
hour, for a short stretch just to be sure I could say it
had gone that fast. The speed was scary, and I never
repeated it, only partly because of my father's dismay
at news of this achievement. Another time, wanting
only the best, I filled the tank with high octane
gasoline, despite the assurances of the gas station
attendant that regular really was all that the four
cylinder low compression engine required.

The greatest challenge to family peace occurred
when Cousin Bob and I, in our parents' absence, drove
the Golden Menace to Sacramento. (They hadn't said
we shouldn't; even in their wildest imaginings they
hadn't thought of the possibility.)

On the way back to Santa Rosa, a tire blew near
Davis. I left the car at a service station there with
instructions to repair the tube and put in a "boot" (a
patch to reinforce the weak place in the wall of the
tire) then came home by Greyhound.

The folks and Ellie picked it up on their way
home from Sacramento. Pop drove the Golden
Menace and Mother convoyed in the family sedan. By
the time they reached Dixon, the tire blew again—I
always said it was because the station hadn't put in a
boot—and Pop and Ellie drove numberless miles on the

rim. It's been over 40 years, but I hesitate to bring up this subject, which is as fresh as yesterday in people's memories, especially in the memories of Pop and Ellie.

CAMP THAYER

The effort to win World War II was employing most American adults the summer I was 16 years old, so there were jobs even for youngsters. That's how I became a junior counselor at Camp Thayer on Austin Creek near Cazadero. Of course, I was not a total neophyte, having helped at a childrens' camp run by our family friend Cath Flinn the preceding summer. Still, this was my first experience on my own, working among "strangers."

They weren't strangers for long. Miss Happy, who was director, Miss Marie, the assistant director, Miss Splash, the waterfront director, and the other members of the staff soon were my friends. I was assigned to a kiosk living group with another counselor and a number of small campers and to duties in the Crafts Department. One of my jobs was to gather wood and prepare the campfire for the evening program. I was proud that only one match was needed to start my fires, and that they gave good light without needing additional fuel.

The camp was in the redwoods, near enough to the ocean for cool nights but protected from wind by rugged mountains of the coast range so that days were warm. It nestled between a steep hillside and a great curving stretch of Austin Creek, a location well insulated from intruders. One slow-moving reach with a sun-drenched sandy shore was dammed to make a swimming hole.

In honor of my stepping out on my own, Aunt Phyllis lent me her camera, which I had long admired. It had a bellows and so could be adjusted for photographing near subjects; it even offered a choice of shutter speeds. Everything photographic seemed expensive, but I bought two 12-exposure rolls of film to be sure I'd have enough. Most of the pictures turned out less than perfect despite which—perhaps even *because* of which—they remain a lasting, powerful reminder of that summer at Camp Thayer.

What is most striking about those pictures–about that experience–is how naïve, how innocent we were. It was not that life was easy; it wasn't. It was that even into their mid teens youngsters still were children. No amount of money, no protection, nothing could command that treasure today.

Camp life was replete with new experiences. There were cookouts at the beach on cook's day off, and I learned to flip a flapjack, sending it into the air with an experienced flick of the wrist and catching it other side down as it fell. We baked pie in a reflector oven, fried eggs on hot rocks, made "axlegrease" (peanut butter and grape jelly) sandwiches. For more formal meals, we sat at the tables in the dining hall, eight or ten people at the sides and a counselor at each end, one to serve and the other to scrape plates.

We sang grace before meals, shared new songs at

top-Miss AJ holds pies ready to go into the reflector oven. (Note the photographer's shadow.)
below-The camp handymen and the "old truck."

evening campfires, and I learned to blow taps on the bugle. We swam, hiked, played games, and enjoyed outdoor living, with stars at night and occasionally even a little morning fog.

And the fragrance of the earth. Unforgettable! Departing, a part of the place goes with us, a part of ourselves abides. Sometimes even now I dream I'm walking from the kiosk to the washroom, toothbrush and towel in hand. To this day, that bouquet of loam and meadow in the morning dew is as real as if I were there.

Some of the senior campers were as old as I was. I would have liked to count them as friends, but I was an organization person well satisfied with the status quo whereas they were a generation ahead of their time, with a lifestyle characterized by the expression, "Question Authority."

They were an innovative lot and leaders in whatever they did. Their role as the guiding force of the Thayer Thespians led to the smash hit dramatic production of the summer. When the cast was half way through rehearsals for the play that the drama counselor had chosen, the seniors declared it was passé; they'd rather do a parody on the musical, "Oklahoma." Miss Bert was a straw in the wind before their united determination.

The central theme was a romance between the handyman and Miss Happy (in real life twice his age). Of course most of the actors were seniors, but they persuaded even the Camp Director to take a small part in the play.

top-Thayer Thespians in scene from summer play
below-"Sophisticated" Seniors 1944 style.

Everyone went around camp for days humming the lyrics about the ancient service vehicle, sung to "The Surrey with the Fringe on Top."

Watch those kids and see how they scatter
When they hear that old truck's clatter,
Busy folks get madder than a hatter,
A place to hide they hunt.

Oh the body is gray and the wheels are black,
The dashboard's genuine tin.
Ain't got no top to keep out rain, but it's easy
to climb in.

That also was the summer that I—we—got lost. The incident started one warm evening when three of us, a senior counselor, a camper and I climbed the hillside behind camp to pick huckleberries.

We were rushing to get just a few more when one of us realized, "The fog's coming in. We'd better hurry back to camp."

The berry bushes were in a little clearing. As soon as the path left it and entered the trees, we were in trouble. Our one weak flashlight barely showed the stretches of trail that were well-marked. We lost it altogether when we reached a section that was faint.

This part of the coast range is rugged and steep in contrast to the gentle stream valley where the camp was located only a fifteen or twenty minute walk away. We were moving along at a virtual crawl when the one in the lead said, "We're right at the edge of a cliff. I'm scared!"

We all were frightened. The hill plunged into vacant darkness. With luck and daylight one might find her way down. It would be folly to try it at night.

"I think we should stay right here till morning," the senior counselor advised. "No one will miss us; none of us had duties tonight."

"Yes," I echoed. "We'll go down as soon as it's light and hop into our beds for an hour or two before reveille."

Talk about discomfort! The ground was hard, sloping, and chilly. We took turns "sleeping" in the middle, which was the least cold of three icy positions. And we got up at first light to sneak into camp.

Unfortunately someone had missed us. When we walked in at dawn it was to be confronted by the Camp Director and the Assistant Director who, once they were sure we were unhurt, were exceedingly annoyed. We really didn't blame them, though we thought that staying put had been the right thing to do under the circumstances.

Actually, the incident couldn't have turned out better in the end for me. Now that I was under a cloud with the authorities the seniors decided that I must be OK. One of the leaders, Betty, even offered me advice. "You didn't do anything wrong," She said. "*Never* apologize." I didn't.

By then the summer was nearly over. In just a few more days the campers left, and the staff remained to close up. The undertaking was a far bigger job than usual, because we had to inventory the camp for the first time. The Director invited Betty to stay on as a junior counselor to help. She and I were assigned to work together, a partnership that has led to our lasting friendship.

In typical modus vivendi, the inventory started with a pep talk "for the good of the group."

Miss Happy addressed us, "What ho! Staff! Next summer Marin County will move to a new location. Sonoma County will keep this one. So!.....we'll count our possessions, and the Camp Fire boards can total the assets and make a fair division.

"Miss Splash, will you please do the waterfront? Miss Marie has offered to help with the Crafts Department. Cookie and I will do the kitchen."

"Miss Edith and Miss Betty, *Your* job is to inventory the storehouse. Take these clipboards and plenty of paper. It's a big undertaking, but I know you can be counted on to do it well."

She paused for a moment. Betty and I didn't want to admit we'd never inventoried anything before; still, we needed to know.

"What do we inventory?" I asked.

"Everything," Miss Happy said. "We need a complete tally of everything in the storehouse."

We were determined to do a good job. We wore our Sunday white shorts and blouses and our polka dot junior counselor neckerchiefs. And we had red bandanna "sit-upons" attached to our best handwoven belts.

We got our first inkling of the size of the job when Betty unlocked the door. "Wow!" She said.

"Crammed full! We need a plan. We'll make a line down the middle and each take one side."

"I wonder if we should dust things as we go?" I asked.

"I think so. It certainly *needs* dusting, and that way we won't have to come back and do it afterward. We'll use our sit-upons," she said, untying hers from her belt. "After all, we won't be sitting at this job."

"I suppose we ought to develop a format, put everything in the same order for easier reading," I suggested. "Would it be better to write 'axehandles - 1' or '1 - axehandles'?"

Betty, whose dad was in the insurance business, was more accustomed to ledgers and forms than a child like me whose parents were school teachers. She thought "1 - axehandles" preferable. "And we also should mention condition," she suggested.

Almost immediately I found another. So the list now read "2 - axehandles: 1 new, 1 broken." I dusted them and moved on.

By noon we'd gotten well into our job. Our sit-upons were black with grime, and we had lost our morning freshness.

When the 5-minute warning gong rang for lunch, we raced to our kiosks, grabbed toilet articles, and hastily washed up. We hardly need have bothered. Everyone was so pre-occupied with her own contribution to the work that our wet- and dirt-streaked faces occasioned no comment.

After lunch we got right back to work. Our lists by now were impressive:

2 - axehandles: 1 good; 1 broken
1 - lawn chair, broken
5 - shovels: 4 good, 1 broken handle (blade OK)
1 - sledgehammer, handle broken
3 - brooms: 1 used; 2 worn out
And so on...............

"It seems as if a lot of this stuff is broken," Betty observed.

"Yes. But I'm sure they'll want to know about it. After all, won't they need to order replacements?"

"I suppose so," Betty agreed.

"What about these nails," I asked, as we came on several cans of them toward the end of the day.

"You heard Miss Happy," Betty said. "Include 'em."

We finished just before the dinner gong sounded. Afterwards we showered and put on our second best white blouses and shorts and clean sit-upons. And we carefully copied out the list. Then we went to the director's cottage to hand in our inventory.

"Here it is, Miss Happy," we chorused.

She took it from us and started to study it. To her credit, she never cracked a smile, even when she got to the very end, which read "556 nails, assorted; all rusty; 229 straight; 327 bent."

Graciously, she shook hands with each of us and commended us on a job well done.

A SIMPLE CABIN

A cabin is preeminently a place to share. We like to show our guests the original building and how it has evolved over the years in response to the changing needs of family and friends.

"Margaret's Uncle Harry helped design the extra roof bracing when the cabin was new."

"Margaret used this table for her first aid work at Berkeley Camp in 1925."

"Here are the shelves Rhodes built for the fishing equipment."

"The tank that Cath contributed when we first pumped water is in the attic."

"Rhodes helped the girls build the kitchen ceiling when they were in college and wanted to come up skiing."

"Nephew Bob lined the bunkroom with smooth knotty pine when our twin granddaughters were small, so they wouldn't get splinters."

"The cabin is much warmer and freer from drafts since grandson Vince installed house wrap before we re-shingled."

It was in 1925 that Margaret, our mother, filed on a lot and arranged for Mr. Ward to build.

"What kind of a cabin could we get for $250?" she asked him.

The cabin in 1929.

Mr. Ward thought for a moment. He was a gentle, educated man, a Presbyterian minister. Margaret never knew his history, but there was a sadness about him. He made his living during summers by building cabins.

"My crew and I could build a twelve-by-twenty," he finally said. "That's a common size for proving up on a lease, and it makes very good use of materials. You get a lot for your money." He took a used envelope out of his pocket and sketched a simple rectangular building.

Margaret, whose father often brought home blueprints for his work, was experienced at reading plans. "Twelve-by-twenty feet, I see. There'd be one door in the gable end. Eventually we'd build a fireplace opposite it. No chance for one now, I suppose?"

"No, we'd need to economize. We'd save on labor and materials by constructing with spaced sheeting and shakes for the walls and with a board and batten roof. We'd use rocks for the foundation. We can buy lumber at Meyers and lodgepoles for the stringers and framework near Vade."

"What about the windows?"

"I think we can get glass ones for the front from the old Tallac Hotel. We'd use screen for the back windows."

"It would just be a shelter then, wouldn't it?"

"Yes, but you'd have a good, basic cabin that you could improve as your fortunes rise."

"When could you finish the job?"

"We'd build this fall if the weather holds.

Otherwise, next spring."

Margaret mentally reviewed her savings account. Neither she nor Rhodes had much money put by. She finally said, "Our hearts are set on a place in the mountains that we can call home. I'd like you to go ahead."

Margaret's mother wept when she learned of the plan. "Oh how can you think of such an expenditure?" she lamented. "You and Rhodes will need the money to furnish a house when you're married next summer."

Despite her concern, the Trussells knew their own priorities and never have regretted the investment. In fact they had had this summer home four years before they made the down payment on the house which became their winter home.

The history of our family's settlement began in 1923 when Margaret Brown and Rhodes Trussell worked at a municipal camp near the lake. That was the summer that Margaret accepted Rhodes' marriage proposal and that they both fell in love with the area.

In 1925 when Margaret was again working at the camp, her friend Eloise Dyer said, "Raleigh Bryan [District Ranger] is going to cut some new lots. I'd be delighted to help you choose one."

Margaret liked a waterfront lot across the lake from the main trail, one in a low, lush area beside a stream. But Eloise, who'd had a cabin for several years, suggested, "Pick a higher, drier site and not too far from the main trail. There will be fewer mosquitoes, and you'll have access even when the lake is rough."

"Good idea," said Margaret. "Though such

practical considerations never would have occurred to me."

"Let me show you a place that I like," Eloise said. "It has lake frontage, and it rises to a terrace twenty five feet above the water that would be a good building site. The cabin would get sun in both morning and afternoon.

"There's an ancient, sprawling juniper tree at the front. My children and their friends have used it as a playhouse for years."

Winter came early in the fall of 1925, so Mr. Ward couldn't build till summer. When Margaret and Rhodes arrived July 5, 1926 for their honeymoon, the carpenters were still finishing work.

The newlyweds sat on a rock near the ancient juniper with its branches, some dead and grey with age, others with cinnamon colored bark and bright green foliage. The sun that warmed their shoulders shone from a deep blue Sierra sky. Now they had a cabin of their own where they could share the mountains with friends and family.

It was a time for sharing. Margaret's brother had lent them his new car for the trip. Her sister and brother-in-law had lent their Sacramento home for the stopover enroute.

Finally the workmen nailed the last board and swept out the shavings. Rhodes carried Margaret over the doorstep of their new cabin. They were home.

Life was simple. Rhodes cut boughs for a bed, because the furniture had not come. They lived mainly out of doors in the best tradition of the Berkeley open-air devotees that they were. They even cooked over a campfire. Eloise lent them a hide-away bed and a portable wood cookstove to use indoors when the weather turned cold and rainy.

However, even fresh air advocates need more shelter than the original one room offered. When Rhodes arrived in 1929, there was a snowbank on the floor, so he pulled off the boards and battens and shingled the roof.

Then, with an economy that set an example for many later improvements, he recycled the old materials to construct a six by eight foot kitchen on the gable end opposite the door, where original plans called for a fireplace. (That didn't come till 1958 and then on a different wall.) Friends laughingly dubbed the addition the "Toonerville Trolley," because the leaning stovepipe and rakish roof reminded them of a cartoon by that name.

The family grew and the space expanded. We first built the bunkroom as a tent platform-sleeping porch and later enclosed it. We added an eight by sixteen foot kitchen and dining room in 1935. Finally we constructed a wash-shower-toilet area. The cabin was 240 square feet in 1926 and is 522 square feet plus decks in 1994.

"We still call the original twelve-by-twenty the 'main cabin,'" comments Margaret, "But we now have added double floors, better bracing, solid sheeting on roof and walls, a fireplace on the lake side, and thicker, better insulated walls."

Over the years, the number of family users has grown from two, now in their 90's, to more than a dozen, including children and grandchildren, each allotted time in the schedule. The cabin is rarely vacant from early June till late September. It is not unusual for as many as forty people, including guests, to use it during the course of a summer.

Careful scheduling and conscientious attention to stewardship are essential. One person is in charge of the calendar, with the following priorities: Margaret and Rhodes, still the owners, have first choice of dates and unlimited time (though they usually reserve only two weeks); their three daughters two weeks each; the grandchildren one week each, and some friends who've been coming for years, one week each.

There are certain rules that everyone follows. Sign the guest book. Leave the land, the building and the motors, boats, beds, ad infinitum in good condition. If something breaks, repair it. If in doubt, read the instructions book, which includes such disparate information as how to put up the tent, what to do if you run out of flamo (turn off the empty tank before turning on the full one; otherwise you'll have two half-tanks instead of one full and one empty), how to manage the chemical toilet, how to turn on/off the water supply from the community system.

Probably the shared use succeeds because everyone has a personal stake in the cabin. Family and friends have contributed most of the labor over the years. They've even obtained the materials by helping wreck abandoned buildings, such as avalanche-damaged places and the old Boy Scout Camp. In fact, one of the Trussell daughters quips, "I was in college before I knew boards came from lumber yards and nails didn't have to be straightened before they were used."

A thoughtful viewer can still perceive the twelve-by-twenty nucleus and identify the additions. Rhodes, the principal planner of these changes, was quick to adopt new ideas, including a privacy screen for the wash area. It repeats a style John Davis Hatch, architect-owner of the place next door, introduced.

There are a surprising number of twelve-by-twenties besides ours around the lake, but picking them out requires careful observation. Adjustment to the needs of the owners, not artistry, has concealed their identities. For example, here is a building that started out as a single room; the owners later added an "L" on the back and more recently enclosed a porch. Here is one with the front door at the side, an addition at the gable end and another on the back. This log cabin, the oldest on the lake, is essentially unaltered from its original form.

A cabin mirrors the lives of its inhabitants. Each has its own history, the arcane lore of the people who built it—indeed, who still are building it.

The cabin in 1994.

FOOTPATHS

In 1963 when I first visited the city of Leeds, my English grandfather's birthplace, one of mother's cousins accompanied us to Adel Church. We climbed a stile, followed a footpath through a field of grain, climbed another stile, crossed a road to the little Norman church. Grandfather had taken this same path through this same field to this same church when he was a boy almost a hundred years earlier. How many generations of our forebears had exercised their right to this public way?

Walking was one of grandfather's favorite activities. We children often accompanied him on Sunday afternoons along quiet roads near our then-sleepy town of Santa Rosa, California. He knew a lot about his community—its homes and businesses, its agriculture, its people. I understand better how he came by his love of rambling since a trip to the Cotswolds and Shropshire in April, 1992.

I went there with an English friend. Bette is an inveterate walker; not a day passed but we explored the paths through woods and fields. *Through* them, that is. The public footpaths are long established and jealously preserved rights-of-way over private land. They forge a link between town and country, enabling the wayfarer to see not just the outer boundaries of the countryside but its very fabric, the warp and the woof of the landscape.

Every public footpath is unique, but there are some commonalities. There is an unobtrusive signpost that points the way, a stile to cross a fence, a trace lightly worn in the grass to follow to the next stile, then through the next field and the next.

Footpaths offer an example of co-existence in an increasingly crowded world. "Leave only footprints; take only photographs" is etiquette assiduously observed; people leave livestock, crops, and buildings strictly alone.

The entry to most paths, and integral to their success, is a stile. Stiles ease the relationship between farmer and rambler, for there are no gates to open or close, no chance that livestock will escape.

Stiles also can encourage mutual understanding. An elderly lady of waning strength left a note, "This stile is too high." The next time she came that way, she found the farmer had rebuilt it.

There are styles and styles of stiles. Sometimes they are factory-made turnstiles called "Kissing Gates"; push the gate ahead to enter; push it back to exit; people fit through the narrow opening but livestock don't. Sometimes there are stairs to climb one side of the fence and down the other. Or there is a bar at the top of the fence and about half way up each side a protruding board. Step up on the near board; swing a foot over the bar and onto the other board; lift the second foot over and onto the ground.

Bette and I bought an Ordnance Survey map that

The entry to most paths is a stile.

showed public footpaths, iron age hill forts, long barrows, and much more. The hostess at our farmhouse bed-and-breakfast studied it with us and suggested favorite walks.

We stepped out the door, followed the road a hundred yards, turned up a muddy farm track, crossed a stile, and started over the hill to the village of Upper Slaughter. The path bisected a grassy sheep pasture. The ewes hardly spared us a glance; people were no surprise to them.

It was Easter week; wherever we went, we met other ramblers. There were infants in perambulators, oldsters, families, even backpackers on extended tours. There was plenty of room; people passed with a smile and a "cheerio." We had tea and scones at a church fund raiser in one village, fish and chips at a sidewalk table in another, then took the bus back to Upper Slaughter and retraced our steps from there.

Every path explores its own landscape, the special qualities of present land use, the dynamic, living history of its past. Once when the sun cast revealing shadows on a grassy slope, we saw gentle undulating waves, long parallel mounds side by side. They are "old fields," the remaining vestiges of open field farming which was common in the time of Geoffrey Chaucer (the 14th century).

Wherever we went in the Cotswolds we saw sheep. There were lambs in groups of six or eight, adventuring from the ewes but ready to scurry back for protection—or even just to get a swig of milk. The mums were busy grazing, but the babies chased, butted, defended minor eminences in "King of the Mountain" contests.

One afternoon we climbed through sheep pastures to Belas Knep, a "long barrow," or burial mound, atop an imposing hill. Early agriculturalists built it of field stones about four thousand years ago. Archaeologists estimate that the construction, with internal passages, roofed chambers, and drystone faced walls, took as many as 15,000 man hours. Though now it is covered with grass, the white limestone monument must originally have been a beacon to the people in the fields and villages below.

Another time we visited Offa's Dyke, named for the English king who had it constructed of rocks and soil about 800 A.D., a time of castle building and fortification along the Welsh/English border. Personnel at the Information Office near Knighton gave us instructions for reaching the best preserved part.

The purpose of this earthbank, which is up to 25 feet high and 80 miles long, was to regulate border trade. Alongside it originally was a steep V-shaped ditch hardly a trace of which remains today. Much of this amazing earthworks is on private land and without public footpath rights, but for some twenty years members of the "Offa's Dyke Society" have been working to preserve it and make it available to all walkers.

Villages, fields, animals, earthworks—Grandfather was right. I returned from England with a new understanding of my heritage. Nothing beats a stroll along a public footpath for getting to know the land.

ADVENTURING
IN YOUTH HOSTELS

"The Rocky Mountains!" Bette said, "We could stay in youth hostels."

Youth hostels!

Well, OK; I'm past my youth, but I'll try anything once. It was great! Hostel life proved inexpensive, challenging, and a unique opportunity for sharing.

Inexpensive! (All prices are as of 1991 and, except at Polebridge, Montana, in Canadian dollars.) The cost per night per person for members (annual membership $25) ranged from $8 to $14 depending on accommodations. There was no need to eat out, for all hostels had self-service kitchen and dining areas stocked with cookware, utensils and stoves. Big ones like Banff, which can accommodate 150 guests, also provided luxuries like sitting areas, telephones, showers, and electric lights.

Challenging! The dorms were never noisy, but they were crowded ranging from four people per room in double bunks up to, in one instance, twenty one in triple deck bunks. Too, I'm a fresh air fanatic, whereas most bedrooms were warm and with windows closed.

Sharing! The Rocky Mountains, their steep slopes and stark heights, were wonderful. But ah! the people—The people were unforgettable. Especially at small hostels in remote areas we quickly got acquainted.

Travelling Companion. Bette is a perfect traveller, knowledgeable about the world and quick to find common ground with other people. She also speaks French, an accomplishment that widened our horizons. And her gourmet stir-fry assured us of excellent quick meals.

Exploring The Rockies. We hired a car at Calgary airport. Our plan was to drive straight to Jasper then return by the same route over the following two weeks. Then we'd spend a few days in Glacier Park, Montana, and finally back to Calgary and home.

The road north followed valleys. We caught glimpses of glaciers and saw streams clogged with glacial debris. Mountains towered over us, mountains composed of layer upon layer upon layer of sedimentary strata warped and uplifted by tectonic forces and graded down by erosion.

We had a closer view of the strata a few days later from the aerial tram up Whistlers Mountain. There were jumbles of weathered boulders looking as if at any moment the mountainside might crumble. That judgment seemed to be confirmed by the landslide at Crowsnest Pass which we saw toward the end of the trip.

Maligne Canyon Hostel (capacity 24) was our first and most rigorous experience. We carried water from the nearby stream and boiled it for five minutes before use. There was no refrigerator. The toilets were pit privies.

Trotter, the hostel manager, signed in new arrivals and explained the rules—wash your dishes promptly; help with tasks for half an hour in the morning; quiet and lights out in the dorms after 10 p.m. At first we thought him overly managing, but we later appreciated that this initial emphasis on organization kept things running smoothly to everyone's benefit.

Trotter was more than a "manager"; he was the host, eager to smooth the way for his guests. Late one evening he came to the multi-purpose cabin to invite everyone to see the aurora borealis, the "Northern Lights." They lasted about five minutes, extraordinary luminescent mother-of-pearl streamers against a black velvet sky. Seeing them was our very good fortune; many visitors never do.

When a ranger spotted harlequin ducks near Maligne Lake, Trotter took two of the guests to observe them early the next morning. Seeing the only North American "torrent duck" meant as much to Bruno and Andrew as the aurora borealis meant to Bette and me.

The focus, node and center of a hostel, and the secret of its success, is the hearth, where the guests break bread. People begin drifting in toward evening, cooking separately but eating side-by-side at the long tables. Most use quick and simple one-dish meals requiring minimal space. Across from my stir-fry is spaghetti; to the left, pork and beans; a neophyte asks the room at large how to prepare macaroni and cheese.

After dinner the hearth, the multi-purpose cabin,

is the sitting place. People read, write, mend, discuss where they're going, tell where they've been, recommend what to see and what to skip.

There was a wealth of field trips to recommend. Such features as disappearing streams and lakes without surface outlet are common near Jasper. We saw a remarkable example of solution when we took the guided nature walk alongside the Maligne River where it plunges down its narrow channel deeply incised into the limestone.

It was also near Jasper that we first saw "glacier milk." Light reflected by fine "rock flour" suspended in the water turns lakes and streams a lovely bright blue.

Bette and I stayed at Maligne Canyon six days, which made us "old timers." We met some remarkable people.

One evening two sisters in their twenties walked in, shook hands all around, introducing themselves to each person. Vigorous, friendly, tanned, they were the epitome of their vast pioneering homeland, travelling ambassadors of good will from Australia. They stayed three nights, then shouldered their backpacks and headed east on the next leg of their odyssey, hitchhiking around the world.

We were concerned for the safety of another hitchhiker, a young French school teacher travelling alone, though she assured us that when a car stopped, she always looked it over carefully and said "thank you, no" if she felt uneasy. She said that one day a motorist on his way to a family reunion invited her to come too. She had an unforgettable weekend as guest of his

Canadian family.

It was at Maligne Canyon that we got acquainted with Andrew, an Englishman, and his Quebecer friend, Bruno. They had worked in a bird refuge in England. Bruno was learning English, having been taught only French at home.

The language problem has its roots in history. Bruno spoke as if it were yesterday of the tragedy of families separated when they were removed to Louisiana by the English in 1755. Today's tragedy is that young Quebecers like him lack the language skills they need in a widening world.

Our next hostel was Hilda Creek, just off the Parkway, near the Columbia Icefield. Enroute we stopped at Athabasca Falls, where a glacier once carried away big chunks of rock as it moved down slope, leaving in its path "glacial rock steps" very different from the smoothed surface characteristic of stream erosion.

Columbia is the largest ice field south of the Arctic circle. Exhibits at the Interpretative Center there show how glaciers radiate outward, re-shaping the landscape by widening and deepening existing drainage into U-shaped valleys with tributary "hanging valleys."

Athabasca Glacier, just across the road, provides hands-on experience. We walked only a few hundred feet on the ice and that *very* carefully. A few weeks earlier a teenager who fell into a crevasse froze to death before rescue workers could get him out.

Hilda Creek Youth Hostel, has room for just twenty one people in one dorm. Gordon, the manager, hadn't much hair, and what he did have he wore in half a dozen straggly pigtails. He seemed relaxed and caring, unflappable, the right man to run a *small* hostel in a location with *big* demand.

He assigned us places in the dorm with tripledeck bunks, where every possible bit of floor space also had mattresses to accommodate the overflow. Even under such crowded conditions, people are considerate, and nights are restful. A bicycling group of a dozen teenagers and two adult leaders shared with the rest of us; the quiet was awe-inspiring.

Hostel managers take people in if they possibly can. A family of four who arrived late and without a reservation slept on the floor in the multi-purpose room.

It was at Hilda Creek that we heard about the remote Whiskey Jack Hostel (named after a bird) in Yoho National Park, especially interesting to us because it is at the trailhead for the famous Burgess Shale. We had reservations at other hostels the next three nights, but Gordon phoned around and got the OK for us to switch. He advised us to go early, because the shortwave radio at Whiskey Jack was out of order, and there was no phone.

The hostel, which is several miles from the main road, occupies a graceful building with handsome pine floors and attractive walls. It used to be the residence for workers at a resort but was made into a hostel (open summers only) after an avalanche wiped out the main lodge.

It seemed luxurious. The water is from a spring,

clear, cool and good. There are propane lights and refrigerator, and the stove has an oven. The bathrooms offer all the comforts of home, even hot showers and flush toilets.

The view from the front porch is spectacular. Yoho Glacier, far to the north, once filled this valley, widening and deepening it, turning it into a characteristic U-shape and truncating tributaries. Takakkaw Falls, one of highest waterfalls in North America, plunges from one such "hanging valley" a short stroll to the east.

We arrived mid morning when most guests were away. Olga, the manager, shared a cup of tea with us at a table on the lawn and told us about the hostel, the area, and herself. She was slim, straight, vigorous, and 69 years of age; she kept young by hiking every day. The summer of 1991 was her thirteenth year in charge of Whiskey Jack.

She had won the award for best youth hostel in Alberta the previous two years, and it wasn't hard to see why. She knew people's names, and cared that they had a good time. She'd added to each bunk a little shelf to hold small items, such as glasses, book, or flashlight. The place was spick and span.

There was a dorm for women, one for men, and one for couples. The only vacant space was in the men's dorm, so Olga assigned Bette and me to it. She invited us to use her own bathroom if the others were busy.

We were there three nights. Once she made cookies to share with everyone; the next day it was a

Whisky Jack Youth Hostel is remote and handsome.

cake; the following evening popcorn, a great kettleful poured into big bowls, one on each table. As soon as she'd dumped one batch she started another, till all of us had as much as we could eat.

Like Trotter, she ran a taut ship. People didn't neglect their KP duties in *her* hostel. And the morning that she discovered a woman setting out a dog's water and food, her ladylike "Are those *my* dishes?" brought a quick apology and speedy replacement with the animal's own bowls.

The Burgess Shale, rich in Cambrian Period fossils of major scientific importance, is a stiff climb up the mountain from the hostel. Bette and I had thought we might hike to it, but Olga said visitors were only allowed in the company of approved guides, because thieves had been caught carrying off gunny sacks filled with the shale.

A retired Canadian Air Force officer was staying at the hostel while attending a seminar on the Burgess Shale. He was glad to spend an evening eating popcorn and talking about his experiences with those of us who were interested. When he visited the site, a university field class was working there. He estimated that 25% of the rock they handled contained fossils.

There are three rich strata, each separated from the others. Extreme pressure when the sediments were uplifted destroyed all trace of once-living organisms in most rocks, but a reef protected these treasures. The fossils date from about 520 million years ago and provide much new evidence on invertebrates.

From our base at Whiskey Jack, we also drove to

"Moraine Lake" (actually dammed by a huge rock slide) and to Lake Louise. Both were "improved" with walks, buildings, and other amenities. They were lovely, but we prefer our mountains wild.

We went next to Banff and spent a night in the huge hostel there. It was pleasant but not memorable. We replenished our food supplies at a supermarket, did some sightseeing, and departed the next morning.

Our next objective was Glacier National Park, Montana. We spent one morning just inside the west entrance at the little shops and along the shore of magnificent Lake McDonald, which is dammed by a moraine. Another day we drove to Logan Pass over the narrow Going-to-the-Sun road, where cliffs plunge down to a valley far below.

The North Fork Youth Hostel in Polebridge, Montana, is 25 miles by gravel road north of the west entrance to the park. Unlike most of the hostels where we stayed, it is privately owned.

The kitchen in the big rambling house is well supplied with pots and pans. There is plenty of work space and a diagram shows where everything belongs. John, the proprietor, has posted numbers of 3 x 5 cards with instructions, such as one that admonishes people to be careful when turning on water at the kitchen sink if anyone is in the shower.

Two young men keep the place up and the dishes done. They also help manage the loan-or-rent equipment, which includes canoes, bicycles, and skiing gear.

Polebridge was larger before a fire in 1988

destroyed twenty five buildings. Only the saloon, the mercantile store, the hostel, and a few houses survived. The pole bridge for which the village was named was destroyed.

Two University of Montana forestry professors were studying the burn. They blamed a century of "no fire" policies for the extreme heat and destructiveness and told us that there still were no small ground squirrels even after three years had elapsed.

Everyone's concerns about grizzlies was heightened by news that one had attacked a tourist. The professors pointed out that wild animals lose their respect for humans where hunting is prohibited, so large carnivores in parks may be very dangerous. Some people think that bells and similar noisemakers are a bad idea if bears regard humans as prey.

An extreme example of such danger occurred in the past in what is now southern Alberta. Indians there customarily placed their dead on elevated burial platforms. Bears that raided these developed a taste for human flesh and became so dangerous that the Indians left. White settlers therefore entered a land devoid of people but frequented by man-eating carnivores.

Polebridge demonstrated once again that hostels are home like. Bette and I heard a lot about "huckleberries," so we decided to pick some. "Old timers" at the hostel found patented scoops for harvesting, gave us little buckets to put the berries into, and told us where to go. Accustomed to western huckleberry bushes, which are evergreen and bear

small, tart berries, I was surprised that these bushes
were deciduous, and the fruit looked and tasted like
domesticated blueberries.

We celebrated the harvest at Polebridge Saloon
known for gourmet food served simply. The chicken
curry was a bit hot, but the celebrated pie al la mode
was ambrosial. The fruit seemed almost fresh
(uncooked). One of the young men at the hostel
worked in the saloon kitchen; he, with great pride,
shared the recipe, which included honey, brown sugar,
flour, and two cups each of berries and sliced peaches.

The last night on the road, we stayed at the
Grand International Hostel (accommodates 64) in
downtown Coleman, Alberta. Newly converted from a
hotel, it had only four guests. We got a freshly painted
room with two double bunks and a private bathroom.

We arrived quite late, delayed by a storm, but
the manager had stayed to sign us in. He even opened
the kitchen so we could prepare a bedtime snack. He
hoped the "noise" from the first floor tavern wouldn't
bother us and offered earplugs, just in case. Bette
checked out the tavern and reported that there was a
hometown crowd listening to live music. The building
must be well insulated, for the sound was barely
audible from our room.

The next morning in the dining room there was
a young man with wild dark eyes and bushy black hair,
a "Mountain Man" with a modern message. After
doctors proclaimed his injured back incurable, he'd
healed himself by taking mega-vitamins and living alone
on the prairie in a canvas covered shack through a sub-

zero winter.

Calgary was next. Enroute, we stopped at Crowsnest Pass where in 1903 eighty two million tons of limestone rock slid off a mountainside, wiping out part of the town of Frank (population 600), and killing an estimated seventy people. Only twelve bodies were recovered.

The scar on Turtle Mountain and the immense rockpile, including boulders as big as houses, are still clearly visible, lighter colored than undisturbed rock. We thought about the rubble on the flanks of Whistlers Mountain and about the slide that dammed Moraine Lake.

We left the rental car at the Calgary airport and returned to the Travelodge where we sorted and packed for the trip home. On the hotel shuttle we met a couple from Texas who glowingly described their trip to the Rockies, complete with luxury accommodations and views of all the important beauty spots.

They did not ask about our experiences, and we didn't attempt to describe the joys of hosteling. We didn't tell them what they'd missed for fear we'd spoil their fun.

THOSE MALLARD DUCKS
The Human Perspective

"Quack! Quack! Quack!" resonated the voice of my sister Ellie.

"Quack! Quack! Quack!" replied our mallard ducks as they flew up from the Santa Rosa Creek, where they spent their days swimming and foraging, to our back lawn to eat their dinner.

We got the ducks in 1935. Our grandfather, who was a sculptor, was carving a phoenix for the family cemetery lot of the Ukiah artist, Grace Hudson. Mother brought Ellie and me along when she took him to discuss plans for the project, and Mrs. Hudson gave us eight cheeping brown and yellow ducklings. We carried them home in a shoebox.

Our father was a farm boy and knew how to care for young animals. "We'll make a brood box so they'll be warm at night," he said.

He fixed one by nailing narrow strips of an old wool blanket to hang down nearly to the floor beneath an inverted box. Till the ducklings grew big enough to take care of themselves outdoors, they slept cuddled together in this snug bed.

The mallards seemed to fit right in with our dog, cats, bantams, and other pets. But Ellie and I were not prepared for their aquatic ambitions. They were nearly grown by the time of the first heavy rains that winter, and when the creek rose they disappeared into the flood.

"Our poor little ducks!" We cried, "They've probably drowned or washed away. We'll never see them again!"

Finally Pop couldn't stand our distress. He took a handful of grain and went after them. Goodness knows how he did it, but after awhile we saw him returning along the opposite bank with a bulging gunny sack fastened over his shoulder. There was no bridge across that part of the creek, only a cable of the old footbridge which had fallen down years earlier. With typical derring-do he crossed the flood hand-over-hand on the cable to drop the precious pets at our feet. We were filled with joy for our ducks and with pride for our father.

Of course, as soon as we opened the sack the ducks went back into the water. This time Pop refused to go after them.

The mallards' independent streak sometimes had less fortunate outcomes. One rainy morning Mother answered the door to find a neighbor from up the block, a big beefy man puffing hard and very red in the face. "Those mallards were slurping through my new onion patch," he said, "turning it into a mud hole."

What *can* you say when "I'm sorry!" seems so inadequate?

The mallards were right at home along our creek and soon became a self-perpetuating flock with their own customs and prerogatives. The adults would nest, sometimes near the water or occasionally in our back garden. By the time my youngest sister was three years old, there often were mothers with their broods on the lawn.

"You must leave the ducklings alone," Mother said. "You'll frighten them if you get too near."

Our small sister, of course, slipped out one morning and picked up one of the babies. The mother promptly grabbed Marian by the front of her overalls and thrashed her with its wings. The child's screams outdid even those of the duckling. Ellie and I thought the punishment served her right. Our parents, despite our reservations, rescued her.

The nesting period was special. Early in the spring when winter floods had scoured the creekbed clean of last year's debris and buds on streamside plants were at their most tender and insects and other delicacies at the zenith of food supplies for raising wild children, we'd know it was time to watch.

Within a few days of observing them without really appearing to be interested in mallard affairs, we'd usually find a nest. Then we'd check regularly, counting the eggs and guessing when the duck would start to set. Our parents made sure that we didn't disturb them as we observed the progression from freshly laid to new baby, and sometimes we even were lucky enough to see a little one extricating itself from its shell.

Now and then an egg would be left in the nest when the family had gone. These relics usually were rotten, but once we found one that was still alive. We lined a shoe box with flannel and put it in a warm place above the kitchen stove till the duckling could hatch, but we soon decided the baby was not going to break out by itself.

No doubt we should have left the egg alone; instead Ellie and I gently broke the shell away. To our surprise, and to our parents' dismay, a large part of the yolk was still attached outside the baby's body. Apparently the duckling had not been ready for the outside world. Amazingly it survived. We named it Julius, because it was caesarian-hatched, and we took loving care of it.

Julius was imprinted on humans, what with being hatched and cared for by us. Even when he became older, he still would stay in the back garden and run from the other mallards when they came up to feed. When he attained adult plumage and we discovered he was a "Julia," not a "Julius," she still feared ducks.

It was fun at first, but we soon tired of having a duck follow us around. It was no use trying to persuade Julia to go to her own kind, for she believed *we* were her kind. Finally we dropped her from a high retaining wall into the creek near the rest of the flock. She couldn't get back where we were, so she had to try her luck with them. In this drastic fashion she surrendered her residence in the back garden and adjusted to life as a mallard.

Julia was not the only medical emergency involving the ducks. One day after some youngsters down at the creek had been throwing rocks, Ellie found one of the females with a broken thigh. Pop was afraid it couldn't be mended, but he said he'd try.

He plucked the feathers off the injured limb and did his best to splint it with a tongue depressor and bits of tape. She stayed quietly in the garden till her leg healed. Ever after that, she got around quite handily, though she always had a lopsided waddle.

Nowadays when I see mallards in the creek or at the park, I wonder if they're descendants of the ones we brought home from Ukiah in a shoe box. I hope so. I'd like to think that those ducks are still part of the Santa Rosa scene.

THOSE MALLARD DUCKS
The Avian Perspective

June, 1935

Dear Mother,

We had a good ride safely cuddled together in our spacious shoe box. Nobody got car sick. The children are nice playmates. They walk on two legs, just like us.

The accommodations are good and the food excellent. We eat cordon bleu chicken mash—all we want, whenever we are hungry. The bug and worm supply also is abundant, tasty and nutritious.

You'll be glad to know we haven't forgotten about water. There is a nice pool on the lawn where we go paddling. There's also a creek nearby, but we haven't had much opportunity to explore it yet.

We were shocked to discover that the children can't swim! We'd soon teach them if we could, but their parents never allow them to go to the creek alone. Mrs. MacBugTussle plans to have a family outing there soon, so perhaps things will change.

Our people have two cats and a dog. Those animals grow very strange feathers. And extraordinary as it may seem, they have four legs instead of the proper two that Mother Nature gave to ducks and people. They certainly look peculiar, but otherwise they're pleasant enough and good companions.

We're fine. Best to the family.

Love, Mattie x her mark

Transcribed by Robert Robin, Society of Outdoor Amanuenses.

July, 1935

Dear Mathilda,

Things here in Ukiah go along about as usual. All of your brothers and sisters send their best. We didn't lose a single one from your brood, truly an unusually good year.

I'm glad that room and board are acceptable at your new home. Avoid gluttony; overweight makes for poor flight capabilities.

Water is essential to gracious living. Don't give up. Expand your horizons. Plan regular trips to the creek. I just quack my instructions and find that ducklings follow me right in with no discussion or back-quack; you should be able to manage the children easily.

Beware of dogs, cats, skunks and raccoons. Many four-legged beasts are sly and undependable. An adult mallard usually can overcome any cat foolish enough to challenge it, but you need to remember that ducklings are helpless before them.

The larger predators are a menace to all of us.

Why just last month a small dog ate your Uncle Toby. The best policy is to be on guard against all four-legged creatures. Do urge the family to be vigilant.

All here send their regards.

Love, Mother

January, 1936

Dear Mother,

We've had the most extraordinary adventures! With all this rain, the creek rose and Mr. MacBugTussle opened the gate to the poultry yard so the chickens could get to high ground. We ducks, of course, prefer *low* ground. "Wetter is better," as you always told us.

Well! The flood was irresistible. We swam downstream investigating coves and eddies, catching fish and some of the most delectable bugs I'd ever eaten. Of course we mostly avoided the main current as you taught us. No sense in whirling along out of control.

We'd just found a nice place beside the creek where we could rest and preen our costumes—no soggy plumage for your children—when along came Mr. MacBugTussle with a pocketful of grain. We never can resist such a treat. But his intentions were hardly honorable, for as we supped, he picked us up and dropped us into a gunny sack. How humiliating!

Then he carried us, wings, heads, feet all jumbled together and dumped us on the ground in front of his crying children. Their tears turned to smiles when they saw us.

From a duck perspective the only good part of the whole business is that here we were back at our starting point with no effort by us and could repeat the journey over again. Only the second time we had to return upstream under our own power, as Mr. MacBugTussle said once was enough.

During the flood we were free to go and come as we pleased, so we took the opportunity to explore. There are excellent bugs in a garden just down the street from our house, especially delicious because of a slight oniony tang.

We quacked our thank-yous, but the man who lives there is very inhospitable. In fact, he even shook his fist and shouted something about roast duckling, which sent us scurrying home as fast as we could waddle.

Love, Mattie

February, 1936

Dear Mathilda,

Never! Never! Never trust strange people. More than one unwary mallard has ended up roasted or even as duck soup. The man down the street may have designs on you. Beware!

If you children hadn't left home at such an early age, I would have instructed you in survival skills. I'm afraid you are much too credulous.

Love, Mother

P.S. I am pleased to see you've now learned to write. It's never a good policy to trust your personal correspondence to a robin.

March, 1936

Dear Mother,

The most amazing transformation has taken place in our plumage recently. It started with a strange exhausted feeling. Then our feathers began falling out. Some of us couldn't even get off the ground for several weeks. It was terrifying! We all were afraid we were being sacrificed for feather dusters. Shocking! We're not even one year old.

When I was in the depths of despair I suddenly wakened one morning, and there were some fresh, new pinfeathers. Of course all those shafts pushing in tickled terribly. Sometimes I'd get a fit of the giggles and hardly be able to quack.

But I didn't mind even that. What a delight to be properly clothed again. Now we all have new wardrobes, even those whose old costumes had gotten quite rag-tag. The drakes, such egotists, exchanged their juvenile outfits for snappy blue, white, and grey costumes. We ducks also are very attractive though in a less flamboyant way.

I heard Mr. MacBugTussle telling his daughters "That way you can see which are males and which are females. The sex determines the plumage." What does that mean?

Love, Mattie

March, 1936

Dear Mathilda,

We all are pleased to hear that you are becoming big grown-up ducks. Heredity will tell you all about the delightful experience of procreation and of raising a family when it is the right season for that.

In time I am confident that our clan will control the entire Sonoma County, as we mallards are a prolific race and very public spirited. You should begin to think of who might be a good candidate for county supervisor. What about your uncle Millard Mallard? He is quite well known and respected.

Let me know when there are grandchildren, and I'll send them little gifts—I think engraved cups are always nice, don't you?

Love, Mother

June, 1936

Dear Mother,

Well, you were right. First there was the laying of eggs day after day. Then there was setting on them during their egghood to keep them warm and turning them so the embryos would develop properly. Now I am the proud mother of seven wonderful ducklings.

But you *should* have warned me about

internecine rivalries. When I brought my beautiful babies to the creek for their first swimming lessons—you'll be glad to know that they took to the water like ducks—my sister, their Aunt Magnolia, attacked little Marvin. She said he'd ventured too close to her big, overgrown brood.

If I hadn't had the presence of mind to grab one of her juvenile delinquents, I think she might have drowned Marvin. However, I am being more careful now and I have on several occasions taken the opportunity to thrash some of my nephews. Nowadays they keep a good distance from me and mine.

There is a very peculiar duck named Julius in this neighborhood. He thinks he is a human being! Can you imagine that? I heard Mrs. MacBugTussle tell Mr. MacBugTussle that he's "imprinted." I'm sure that's the term she used, but I looked him over from stem to stern and couldn't see a word on him.

Love, Mattie

August, 1936

Dear Mathilda,

The grandchildren must be beautiful, for we mallards are a handsome race. I'd love to see them. Your father and I talk of flying south for the winter as many others do. He is so set in his ways I'll only believe we're going when we actually take off. We'll be sure to drop in on you if we come your way.

You must stand up for your rights with Magnolia,

but don't be too critical. She means well, but she was a difficult duckling to raise and caused me endless worry. Even when she was an egg, she'd roll out of the nest or be a bump in the clutch so that setting was very uncomfortable.

About Julius—I'm sure invisible ink is the answer. Try dipping him in lemon juice. That should bring out the message.

I ordered a silver cup for each of the grandducklings. I chose the ones with a delicious duckweed and dragonfly motif encircling the baby's name. Have they arrived?

Love, Mother

CONVERSATIONS WITH PARKER

When I say that Parker is "my dog," it is an expression of relationship, not of possession. He is my dog in the same sense that Ellie and Marian are "my sisters," or Vince is "my nephew."

The phone rings. It's a neighbor from down the street. "Did you know Parker's out?"

I glance at the front garden. Parker is sleeping in the sun, lying on his favorite patch of iceplant near the gate, asleep with eyes half-lidded, alert to any disturbance that might require his attention. Why is it that people always think it's Parker roaming around when there are six lab look-alikes on Whaleship Road?

There's Bumper Glakeler, Sadie Glakeler, Sylvia Peters, who flunked out of Seeing Eye training because she wasn't assertive. There's Pasquins' Yellow Lab; she's a brood dog for Seeing Eye. And there's a "stranger" that comes on weekends.

And then there's Parker! He *looks* like a Yellow Lab, thick short golden fur with a downy waterproof undercoat that keeps him warm even in the coldest water, floppy ears, soulful Jersey-cow-brown eyes. He weighs in at ninety pounds and stands 24 inches at the shoulder.

On closer inspection, there are some differences between Parker and a lab. His ears lift and tilt forward instead of drooping. His head is broad and massive with plenty of space for the worry lines that furrow his forehead. There's a little curl of coarse golden hair at the tip of his tail. He inherited all that and a powerful physique from his Chesapeake Bay Retriever ancestors. He owes much of his outward appearance to the Golden Retriever side of his family.

Inwardly he is one hundred per cent Chesapeake. The most outstanding difference between Parker and a Yellow Lab is his psyche. Yellow labs are sincere, straightforward; you've only to explain to them what you want, and they'll do their best to oblige. When Linda calls "Bumper, heel!" her lab drops everything and comes running.

Parker is cunning, clever, his thinking convoluted. Explain to him what you want, and he'll weigh all sides of your suggestion. Call him to come home, and he hides behind a bush till he makes up his mind whether or not to postpone breakfast and circumnavigate the neighborhood. At the shore I throw the ball onto the dry sand. He picks it up, looks reproachful as if I were a disobedient, backward child, then detours down the slope and dips it into the water before returning it to me.

When we go for a walk, he pays no attention to me as long as I keep moving. If I stop for a few minutes he checks to see what's wrong and jumps barking, up and down till I get moving again.

Nor does he neglect community service. Even the most distant siren does not escape his notice. His voice, which used to be flat and uninteresting, has matured into a glorious tenor with range, timbre, and volume that would qualify him for a leading role on any opera stage. Outdoors, he effortlessly informs the entire neighborhood; indoors, his voice could rupture eardrums.

He makes the rules of the games he plays. He peers in the window wanting me to come outside. I come; he drops the ball into my hand; I toss it; he runs and grabs it. Now that he has an audience, he dashes back and forth, dodges, feints, checks the shrubbery for intruders, peers out the gate, and brings the ball back only when he perceives that my interest is flagging and I'm about to return indoors.

He has a superb sense of smell and enjoys hide-and-seek retrieving, in which I send him in one direction and throw the ball in another. Around and around he goes till he finds it. Take him in the car; as soon as we stop, he pokes his nose out the window and inhales, identifying, evaluating the place where we are. To Parker, a walk is an olfactory odyssey.

He was born July 19, 1987, and adopted in his puppyhood as a companion to a black lab. When he was six months old, his family advertised in the paper and gave him to me, because, they said, he loved people and needed more human attention.

He and I attended novice dog school, where he proved a challenge to the teacher and to his classmates of both species. Though a quick learner, he advocates autonomy and scorns slavish obedience.

Don't get the idea that he isn't a joy. He is the happiest dog I've ever had, and the least fearful. Even

Parker Trussell tenor, Bette Whelan tin whistlist.

thunder storms don't faze him.

He loves people. At the veterinary hospital, he rushes in, greets all the attendants, wriggles up and down on the scales so that his "weight" fluctuates markedly from one visit to another, stands on his hind legs to examine the pictures on the wall, and happily accompanies the doctor to the back room to have even a painful treatment.

His muscular chest and shoulders swell with power. He's a deer, head up, legs straight, bounding boldly through the brush. He is a lion, head low, tail down, stalking stealthy in the grass.

Swimming is his delight. Throw a ball; he does a racing dive, churns after it, and returns it near to hand then stands watchful to plunge after it again the instant it's airborne. He'll retrieve a stick, too—but balls are in; sticks are secondary—he drops the stick the moment he reaches shore.

Then there's the matter of speech. I must confess that I'm not quite sure whether I understand Doglish or he speaks English. But his body English is excellent. So when I suggested to him that we record a few of our conversations, he readily acquiesced. I think he partly was motivated by the dog biscuits, though he claims it's all for enriching the literary heritage of Bodega Bay.

Miss Kitty

"Pay attention, Parker," I said, establishing a firm grip on his collar. "How can we finish our writing if you won't pay attention and get to work?"

"I've got a lot of other things I need to do today. I think I'll just amble on down the road and see Miss Kitty. How about tomorrow...or next week might be even better?"

"Just pay attention. Look at the notebook."

"I am paying attention," he sighed, turning his face toward the notebook.

It was a classic case of Chesapeake passive resistance. I could tell by the way he looked out the corners of his eyes that though his face was engaged, his mind was through the gate and down the street at Miss Kitty's.

"No! Bad dog! You're not to chase Miss Kitty."

"Don't worry! She likes to be chased. She says it's invigorating. Why her tail stands up like a bottle brush just to see me. She's even trying out several new feinting and dodging techniques."

"Nonsense! Barbara will be upset. She rescued Miss Kitty; that little cat is special."

"Yes, I know. It's a grim tale, too often told. Miss Kitty grew up in a dysfunctional family in

Martinez. Her own folks neglected her, didn't give her love and attention—or even feed her regularly. She seemed doomed to roam the streets going from garbage can to garbage can for her very survival, a poor waif with a short, sad life and an untimely end." Parker pointed his nose to the sky and began to moan, took a deep breath and geared up for a full-fledged howl.

I had to shout to be heard, "It's OK, Parker! No howling! Don't forget her story has a happy ending. Barbara and Robert used to feed her, take care of her, see that she wasn't left to roam the streets. And they liked her so well that they kidnapped her when they moved to Bodega Bay."

He got off one last drawn-out howl, then brightened. "Kidnapped?" He scoffed. "You're confused. She was catnipped."

"The bottom line, Parker, is that Barbara doesn't like anyone to chase Miss Kitty."

"Barbara makes an exception in my case," Parker said. "In fact, I'm her canine hero for chasing that orange cat, the stray that beat up Miss Kitty, injured her so she had to go to the emergency. I chased that bully at considerable personal sacrifice solely because of my devotion to dear Miss Kitty."

"Devotion! That's not how I saw it. We were walking up that steep first pitch of Whaleship Road. We got almost to the turn by Edith's house when we saw the cat. I had a firm grip on the leash, and I told you to sit. You totally disregarded my command, gritted your teeth, bunched your muscles, and ran."

"It was so exciting, I just got caught up in the

moment. All I could think of was avenging the injuries to dear Miss Kitty. You know Chesapeakes have one-track minds. I couldn't help myself."

"You're only half Chesapeake."

"The better half. I have all the characteristics of that fine breed and none of its faults. I have strength, stamina, intelligence, humor, and the courage of my convictions. In short, I am a marvelous dog."

"Stubborn! That's what you are."

"That, too. It's just that I'm always right."

I could see this conversation was getting me nowhere. "Anyway, you were wearing your prong collar and trailing your leash the day you chased the orange cat. I thought that the leash would be sure to snag on something, and the prongs would gouge your neck."

"You were right. They did. Only a really dedicated Chesapeake would have continued the pursuit despite the pain."

"Unfortunately you chased that orange cat through Edith's garden and Ruth and Ira's and down behind Margaret and John's. All those people have nice landscaping. Goodness knows what damage you may have done."

"Don't blame me; I just followed the cat. Besides, I was careful not to step on the plants."

"Fortunately we have generous, forgiving neighbors. We could have been sued."

"You might have been. I don't have a cent to my name. Anyway, I know everyone was glad to have me rid the neighborhood of that pillaging, villainous, orange cat."

"Whatever the case, you just stay away from Miss Kitty. She's special, with her little collar and bell."

"That bell! That bell's an abomination! Miss Kitty can't catch a thing with that around her neck. How can she get proper vitamins and minerals? Why she hasn't had fresh robin in years. She should protest to the ACLU."

"I must admit she doesn't seem to catch anything. Her stalking and pouncing skills have gone to the dogs, so to speak."

"Not *this* dog! Chesapeakes don't need feline facilitation. We're inherently expert at martial arts."

"That's enough argument, Parker. You are not to disturb her."

"Disturb her! Why she's probably waiting under a car beside the road just hoping I'll stop by. She might decide to climb a tree. I could give her a few pointers. I've treed more than one cat."

"When a dog 'trees' a cat, the dog is supposed to remain on the ground while the cat climbs the tree."

"That's how it's done, eh? How dull! I can climb as well as any cat, and it elevates the whole chase to a more sportsmanlike event."

"Dogs don't belong up trees. You should keep your feet on the ground."

"Miss Kitty climbs trees. Anything Miss Kitty does, I can do better."

"Ridiculous!"

He faced in the general direction of Barbara and Roberts' and took a deep breath. "Meow!" He said, "Meow-ow-ow-ow-ow......."

Postscript

"Isn't that book finished yet?" Parker exclaimed. "It's been four years. If you don't hurry it'll be out of date before it even gets into print."

"Don't rush me, Parker. Co-authoring with a Chesapeake isn't easy. We'll just have to add a postscript, bring everything up to date. What changes do you have in mind?"

Parker's tail wagged, slowly then faster and faster as he wound himself into a dance; then he jumped up and down and barked. Then he ran pell-mell around the house. "Jan and John! It happened when they were my house guests. They had such a good time that they went right out and bought a house so they could see me every day."

"They certainly are a fine addition to our neighborhood, though I'm not sure I agree with your interpretation of events."

"Poor Miss Kitty," Parker exclaimed. "Nine lives and she's out!"

"But don't forget that Barbara and Robert now have two new cats."

Parker picked up a tennis ball, one with a hole in it and bit down hard so the air whistled out.   "I wouldn't know.   Chico and Lola haven't had the privilege of meeting me as yet."

"Nor will they, I fervently hope. And what about Ginger?"

"We lost her," Parker said. "But what a splendid achievement! What a wonderful way to go! She threw herself into her work while supervising a tremendous catch of albacore."

"Now Tom has one of Ginger's younger sisters as boat dog," I said. "Izzy'll fit right in. Jack Russells are high spirited."

"Just like me. Jack Russells are Chesapeakes in disguise. I'd be excellent. Look how much more boat dog you'd get for your investment."

"You're too big. Tom sometimes has to carry Izzy while he climbs across several other boats in order to get to his boat."

"You're right about not being carried. I always find that four-on-the-floor makes for ease of investigating, eating, and/or marking, as the particular conditions dictate. But no sense Tom having to do all the work; I could carry him. It's easy—Mom just used to pick me up by my head or the nape of my neck."

"I think he'd probably prefer to go on his own, Parker. But thanks for your offer."

"And that's that!" said Parker. "Now hurry up and get this book to the printer. I want to see my name in lights."

It was clear that his mind was out the gate and down the road.

A FABULOUS HIKE

Most people think that Artemis, Zeus and other Olympians went out of business centuries ago. But in an amazing time warp, the whole lot of them were recently rediscovered residing in a condominium at Lake Tahoe. Parents everywhere will empathize with poor old Zeus trying to maintain his cool in a world turned upside down. Children will recognize the difficulties of keeping up with "all the other kids' parents let them" whilst retaining a hold on their own family resources.

Once upon a bright June morning two sisters set out to hike to the fabled cirque lake belonging to Artemis, goddess of hunting, fishing, and unmarried girls. Though they knew no human ever had been there, they had seen the lake on a map made by USGS sorcerers who'd conjured up images produced by flying saucers.

Great clouds boiled over the ridges that morning, so they took magic cloaks to protect them from the rain. These were made of Nile-On and Plass-Teek by the great 20th century goddess, Technologis, a powerful ally of theirs.

Meanwhile, back at the palace, Artemis was embroiled in one of those Olympian family quarrels, this time with her father, Zeus. Though the sisters were

innocent and ignorant of the quarrel, its outcome would greatly influence their affairs.

"What in the world were you thinking of, Artemis, meddling with the thunderbolts? You know I never allow anyone else to touch them. And you left my workbench in the wildest disorder," he shouted.

"Oh c'mon, it's 1988 A.D., not 188 B.C.; all the modern firearms make noise. I just borrowed one tiny bang to use with my bow and arrow."

"So! You admit it! I've told you to stay away from my workshop. I've a good notion to use a thunderbolt on you."

"Just try it! Stop trying to frighten me with your macho, sexist threats."

He looked at her, her spiked hair, her high topped tennies and pink lycra tights, her fluorescent orange tank top, in contrast to his own cream-colored robes with royal blue trim. "As long as you're representing our Olympian hierarchy, I wish you'd dress respectably."

"A lot you know about fashion. You're outdated. Nobody pays heed to you anymore."

"*You'll* see who's outdated. I'll blast you out of the palace if you don't behave."

"Hunh!" Artemis flounced from the Council Hall leaving Zeus raging about disrespect and insubordination.

"I'll show her who's boss!" He growled as he straightened his workbench.

It took him only a few minutes to decide that it was a lot easier to get back at Artemis by throwing obstacles in the way of the mere humans who were under her protection than it would be to challenge her directly. The sisters' expedition was as good as made for his purpose. He leafed through the *Index of Naiads, Public Works, and Other Lesser Gods* and began some long-distance communications.

Unfortunately for his plan, there was only a busy signal when he tried to call Superies, the naiad of the upper lake. Finally the palace switchboard told him the line was down.

Since she didn't receive a message, Superies smiled on the sisters as they were conveyed by motorboat (another invention of Technologis) to the public landing from whence they took the connecting path to the main trail. No sooner had they reached it, however, than they entered the Region of Round Rolling Rocks, where Zeus's minions already had been at work loosening the footing.

The rocks caused the sisters to slide back two steps for every forward step that they took. They were getting Nowhere Fast when Artemis inspired them to turn around and walk backwards, which they did, reaching the first fork in record time. Here Artemis told them that Zeus was heating up a stretch of granite farther along, intending to fry them, and they should take the steep Triangle Lake route to avoid that fate.

The Triangle path was shaded. Almost at once the sisters were set upon by hordes of winging, stinging, singing Musky-Toes. Technologis had prepared them for such an attack; they anointed themselves with the magical ointment, Diethylmetatoluamide and immediately became so repulsive that the winged scourge buried their beaks deep into the lodgepole pines where they stuck fast with their wings still whirling, so that ever after when the wind blew, people could hear singing in the trees.

The sisters followed the path which branched and wound along the mountain, through woods, past noble juniper and scented sage, to the Haypress crossroads where all routes meet. But Zeus was preparing an even greater ordeal. He drew a black veil of cloud over the sky to conceal his activities from Artemis and limbered up his throwing arm, calculating distance, velocity, and wind shear, and taking aim with small thunderbolts that rumbled and grumbled around distant Mt. Ralston.

The sisters continued along a smooth and level trail, bypassed the Great Fishing Lake, and wandered into a dark grove of limber lodgepoles that concealed the cliff that was their next objective. They almost lost their way in this gloomy forest. Only by using their best woodswomanship and aided by Technologis' orienteering compass, were they able to escape to the other side.

By and by they approached the redoubtable Rocky Ridge that guarded the legendary lake. They toiled upward. As they attained the final fearsome ledge, Zeus got his distance and threw a thunderbolt at the top of the ridge. It narrowly missed the sisters. They retreated to the grove, paused briefly beside a tree with a lighting furrow coiled down its trunk, which Zeus put in their way to remind them of his power, and took refuge, thoroughly chastened, in a little glen.

Here they opened the pack that the younger sister carried around her waist and took out the magic rations, peanut butter on French bread, raisins, cheddar cheese, and apple. No sooner had they eaten than it began to rain. They could hear the drops splatting down on all sides. However, they'd put on their Plass-Teek and Nile-On jackets, so not a drop fell on them. Food, rest, and waterproof raingear restored their confidence and determination.

It was fortunate that the sisters' spirits rose, because by this time Zeus was getting his sights adjusted. He hurled bigger and bigger displays of sheet lightning, forked lightning, and thunder, casting them in rapid succession along the flanks of Mt. Ralston and closer and closer to the Rocky Ridge and the Lodgepole Grove where the sisters had taken refuge.

The sisters counted, "One-thousand-and-one, one-thousand-and-two, one-thousand-and-three, one-thousand and-four, one-thousand-and-five." One mile away.

A jagged fork of lightning like the graph of the Dow Jones average in October, 1987, split the sky. "One-thousand-and...;" the boom reverberated from the Crystal Range. Fortune smiled on the two sisters; Zeus missed. He later insisted that the problem was entirely due to the twinge of pitcher's elbow that he was suffering.

Zeus had exhausted his worst weapons with that big bang, and the rest of his efforts dwindled off toward the Crystal Range, his aim becoming progressively poorer as the day wore on. The moment it was safe to travel, the sisters resumed their quest. Finally they emerged at a ledge atop a cliff above the clouds.

When the mist parted, they could see vast Lake Tahoe, and, nearer by, green Grass Lake. But Zeus had concealed Artemis's lake, hiding it around a turn behind a boulder. It was nowhere to be seen.

Map in hand, they stood perplexed. Suddenly there was the trill of panpipes in a lilting highland tune. Dryads! No doubt friends of Artemis. What could be a better place for the nymphs to dance than a secluded little grove amongst these granite cliffs? The sisters crept toward the sound, over a ledge and past a snowbank. They were nearing the cluster of trees when suddenly a man's head showed from behind a rock. They called, asking the way to the lake.

Instantly the head vanished; the music stopped. Moments later, a dog and a ranger appeared; the Dryads had metamorphosed into these earth guardians. The man carried a long-handled shovel, a sure sign he'd been engaged in deepening the lake. He pointed to the short wave radio in his pack blaming Technologis for the sounds of panpipes. The sisters weren't fooled; they could see scuff marks on the sward where the Dryads had been dancing.

The ranger readily told them the way to the enchanted lake. Sure enough! It was around a bend, past the Dryad camp now metamorphosed into an orange North Face dome tent, and down a slope. There was the circular blue lake with only a ripple to reveal that Artemis had just climbed out following her afternoon skinny dip.

They rested in the white heather on the bank, politely averting their eyes till she left, then circumnavigated the lovely lake. Zeus had spoiled the fishing; they saw only one small trout, and it lay dead on the bottom. He had spoiled the fishing, but nothing could spoil the lake.

Zeus, exhausted from his day's pitching, was taking a short nap on his Olympian throne by the time the sisters left the lake. They had smooth travelling till they got back to the public landing. But the naiad Superies, psyche still smarting from a tongue lashing over the easy start she'd allowed that morning, was ready.

The sisters' venerable father had boated up to give them a ride back to their hut; they espied him from afar. They walked out onto the dock. The younger daughter shouted and the elder waved. But Superies caused the fish to grab the bait in a feeding frenzy. And he trolled around and around a little island, paying no heed to his foot-weary daughters.

Meanwhile, Zeus's arm was sore, and he was very grumpy at dinner. He sent the ambrosia back to the kitchen—said it was burnt at the edges. He refused to speak to Artemis, and changed the subject when Hera asked if she should order a new supply of thunderbolts.

As he was getting ready for bed that night, he said to her, "It just isn't fair. Those modern women have help from Technologis as well as from that upstart Artemis. I gave it my best effort, but I didn't have a chance."

"Don't give up, dear," Hera replied. "Joseph

Campbell is on our side. And not only he, but Ida Egli and the students in English 13, Mythic Themes in Literature!"

"Maybe there's hope after all," he said. "I think I'll read for a few minutes before I go to sleep." He checked the oil and adjusted the wick in his bedside lamp, leaned back and picked up his book.

"What are you reading, dear?"

"'The Turtle.'"

"Aristophanes?"

"No, Ogden."

"Ogden? I think you've got the name wrong, dear. Don't you mean Orion? Orion of Boeotia?"

"No, not Orion, Ogden! Ogden of Nash."

Back at the lake, the hikers were still trying to signal their piscatorial parent who persisted in orbiting the island. "I guess we'll have to walk home," said the younger. "How's your ankle?"

"Darn! Looks like we will. It hurts; that elastic bandage didn't help much."

"That's a shame. Maybe it's time for you to seek another opinion? How about acupuncture? Or I've heard some good things about that shaman who lives in the sixth cabin up the lake from the channel."

AUDITED BY THE IRS

Madge and Dusty MacBugTussle were perched on straight backed metal chairs, the kind that are unyieldingly uncomfortable no matter how a person turns or twists. Over a huge formidable flat-top desk, they faced a middle-aged man with hawk nose and narrow face and more corpulent than one would expect from those ascetic features.

He leaned back in a comfortable swivel chair and stared superciliously at them through his pince-nez. The desk was bare except for a small Internal Revenue Service folder marked "**MacBugTussle**."

The man wore a blood red tie and white shirt and a dark suit with vest and gold watch chain. A little badge pinned to his jacket said, "Hello! My name is Theodore Twitchell, and I am always RIGHT."

Dusty wore his sun tans (the ones that weren't patched; indeed, weren't even in need of a patch), his grey and blue plaid Pendleton, (the new one that Madge and their daughters gave him for Christmas), and his fishing vest, the one with all the pockets. He placed his felt fishing hat on the floor under his chair and nervously ran his fingers through his dark hair.

Madge wore a lovely blue dress (her second best) that just matched her eyes. Her red hair, in a short bob, gleamed in the light from a window behind her.

She leaned toward him and whispered, "Don't worry, Dusty, you'll do fine."

Dusty looked at her and thought, as he always did, that she was beautiful, not pretty, but beautiful and wonderfully intelligent, and what a fortunate man he was to be her husband. A muscle in his jaw quivered as he turned his attention back to Mr. Twitchell.

"Now, we're gathered here to audit your last year's IRS return." Twitchell polished his glasses and emphasized his words. "The IRS is questioning the following parts of your return: 'Miscellaneous expenses,' 'Home office,' and 'Income.' Let's start with the Miscellaneous. Your claim of $430 seems way out of line. Do you have receipts?"

"Yes, indeed! Madge, where'd we put those?"

"You have them, dear. I think they're in your pocket."

"Right," said Dusty, "Just a moment." He stood up and reached into the upper right pocket of his fishing vest, the very top pocket on that side. He drew out a sheaf of papers fastened together with a rubber band.

"Gee, those are the plans for my fish smoker. I wondered where they were." He pushed his glasses into a more comfortable position on his nose and sat down to look at them.

Twitchell slapped the desk with his hand, "We need the receipts."

"Sorry, Mister, I've been hunting those plans for weeks. They got into the wrong pocket. See, I find my fishing vest a very good way to keep track of papers–a pocket for everything and everything in its pocket, I always say. But sometimes..."

"Hurry up!" said Twitchell. His face grew red, and he stood up and leaned across the table, leading with his jaw.

"Dusty, you can study the plans later. Right now we need those receipts," said Madge, hoping that Twitchell wouldn't have a coronary.

"Right!" Dusty put the fish smoker plans (how to make one for $12.99 using an old refrigerator for the box) on the desk and resumed his search.

He went methodically through the fishing vest adding the contents of one pocket after the next to the desk top. "There's 'Home office,' when you want to see it," he said. "And here's...oh, here's...guess you don't want that either."

The desk quickly filled to capacity with a packet of six snelled hooks (size 5 long shank), lambswool hat band with an array of dry flies hooked into it, an automatic reel, half a tuna sandwich green with mold but still wrapped in wax paper. "Hmmn, that can go in the waste basket," he said.

Then there was a fisherman's handwarmer, two red and white bobbers, a Dave Davis trolling spinner rig, a jar of salmon eggs, four bass plugs, chewing gum wrappers, carefully preserved notes and diagrams pencilled on old envelopes, three dimes and a quarter, and other important treasures that a man carries in his fishing vest.

Mr. Twitchell snatched the IRS folder and jumped to his feet, not a moment too soon, for with the next lot of bills marked "paid," the whole pile slid across the desk and began to cascade onto the swivel chair and drop to the floor.

"Look here!" Twitchell shouted. "Either you produce the list now, or I will report that you are willfully and maliciously interfering with an IRS Auditor, preventing him from carrying out his duties."

"Aha! Just the papers we were looking for," Dusty said, pulling cash register receipts threaded on a piece of fishing line out of his lower left pocket. "Here they are, Miscellaneous Expenses, total $430. There you are, mister, and all in chronological order from January 1st through December 31st. See, if you thread them onto an old piece of fishing line, they...."

"Never mind, just let me have them. Why there must be at least 430 of them. Let me get out my calculator."

"There's exactly 922 of 'em," Dusty said. "I counted. See, every time I get a receipt I write on it what I bought and thread it on that line. That way they stay in order, why..."

"Yes, I see," said Twitchell, perched on one of those metal chairs usually reserved for taxpayers and holding his calculator on his lap. He worked for five minutes to interpret the dogeared, water stained bits of paper. "I get the total of $445.67, whereas your figure was $430.00."

"I must have added wrong," said Dusty. "How do I file an amended return?"

"See the people at the front desk about that," Twitchell snapped. "Now, let's take the home office next. Hurry up, man. Are these the papers you need?"

"Yes. Those are the papers," said Madge MacBugTussle. Organization wasn't one of Dusty's greatest strengths, she reflected, though he eventually could locate what he wanted in that fishing vest. Some of Dusty's idiosyncracies required understanding, though most were loveable and delightful.

But Type A personalities were very impatient and even sometimes became quite short-tempered. If Mr. Twitchell weren't so obnoxious, she even might sympathize with him.

"Now! You claim an office in your home."

"Well, not exactly in my home, in my woodshed."

"Your woodshed! Why ever there?"

"Well, a man likes to have someplace to work without cluttering up the house. Madge and I just fixed up the woodshed with a little stove, curtains on the windows, and a good door that keeps out drafts, and a big padlock so my fishing stuff'll be safe when we're not around."

"A *woodshed* is not a home office," Twitchell said with curled lip, believing he had victory in sight. "The law clearly states that an office must not be used for anything else, not storage, not bedroom, not anything but the business."

"I read your instructions book," said Dusty. "My woodshed meets all the requirements."

"Well then," Twitchell pounced triumphantly, "Where do you keep the wood?"

"Oh, is that the burr under your saddle! The wood is stacked outside the garage, handy for bringing into the house."

"And what do you keep in your office? You can't be serious when you write 'Fishing' on your tax return."

"Nothing is more serious than fishing. I keep materials, a vice for fly tying—or actually two vices, in case I need another when one is in use—also rods, reels, nets, line, and everything else a fisherman uses if he's serious about business, such as creels, bait, and waders, to name only a few..."

"Never mind. I get the drift," Twitchell said, with a big grin. "However, fishing obviously is a hobby and does not qualify for a deduction. I'll deny both the 'fishing business' and the 'home office.' Now, let's get at your income."

"OK," said Dusty, "Suit yourself. Of course we'll appeal your decision."

"Perhaps you'd want to look further into the fishing business, Mr. Twitchell," Madge suggested. "I think you'd be saving IRS a lot of energy and expense."

"All right," Twitchell grated, "I'm already late for my next appointment and I haven't even eaten lunch. Suppose *you* tell me about the fishing business, Mrs. MacBugTussle." He scowled at Dusty.

"Very well, Mr. Twitchell, let me explain.

"You see, Dusty always has been greatly interested in fishing. Of course, he's a fine teacher, and a wonderful husband and father to our three lovely daughters. But he'd been thwarted in his need to develop every aspect of his fishing. That side of his multifaceted personality had never fully bloomed.

"Then, last year, he tied the 'Lady Jane Hanigan Fly.' Jane is a school friend of our daughters, though of course we all love her like a member of the family. Well, it made our fortune."

"Yup," said Dusty, "It's the hottest thing on the river. No outfit is complete without a dozen of 'em. I filed for a copyright, of course, put a small ad in several fishing journals, and got so many orders that I had to farm out part of the production."

"But no sweatshop piece work for Dusty," Madge explained, "He has a generous profit-sharing arrangement with his employees. The fly has made a lot of money for everyone involved, and we've been able to buy things we'd never had before—a new car, graduate school for our daughters, and new carpets, to say nothing of the balance in our saving account."

"Money! Lots of money!" Twitchell leaned forward avariciously. "What does the fly look like?"

"Well," said Dusty, "Lady Jane Hanigan has diaphanous wings of the lightest shade of blue. The hackles and tail match the body, which usually is blue, gold, green, white and red.

"I chose those colors primarily because of my undivided loyalty to several institutions—blue because Madge and I are Berkeley grads, green because one of our daughters got a degree from University of Oregon, gold for both the Bears and the Ducks, and of course the red and white are for Stanford. One of our best friends went there—very poor choice, in my opinion, but she did, and those are the colors."

Twitchell, who was an old Stanford grad, got to

his feet, his face as red as his tie. He balled up his fists and looked ready to punch Dusty on the nose. "Stanford Forever," he shouted.

Dusty, for his part, was only restrained by Madge's grip on his arm.

"You'll have to excuse him, Mr.Twitchell. He still thinks in Big Game terms of Cal versus Stanford. But enough of that, gentlemen, let's get back to the business at hand." She sat down between the two.

"All right then," said Twitchell, shrinking back to his usual size. "What if your customer attended some other institution?"

"That's why I said the colors are 'primarily' those. If we need to we always can customize the fly by adding just a muted thread of some other color. Most fishermen, though, are quite discriminating about education. I took a poll, which showed with a margin of error of only plus or minus two percentage points, that 85.6% are graduates from one or another of those three institutions of higher learning."

"Notice, Mr. Twitchell," Madge said, "that our fishing business produced a net income of $112,345.97 last year. That's why we are claiming a home office. Now, I'm sure you want to finish up our case. Here are the income..."

"Never mind," said Twitchell, overwhelmed by MacBugTussle logic and wanting to cut his losses, "I'm sure it's all OK." He didn't even try to look for an additional penalty of $40 or $50, which Auditors usually levy in order for the charges to cover the cost of meeting with the taxpayer.

"Now, Mr. MacBugTussle, if you'd like to pick up your papers, I will report that your return is fully in order."

"Don't get up, Mr. Twitchell," Dusty said, "Please tell me how to file an amended return——those miscellaneous expenses, you know."

CLEANING THE GARAGE

"We really must clean the garage, Dusty," Madge MacBugTussle said. "It's so crowded the girls and I had to leave the car in the driveway."

"Why, there's plenty of room. I put it in yesterday afternoon, no trouble at all."

"Yes, room for the *car,* but not for the people. We couldn't open any of the doors."

"Oh, Madge, be practical. You just stop in the driveway, get the cardboard boxes, put them on the hood, and pull on in. And when you leave, drive out of the garage, transfer the boxes from the hood to the floor, and off you go. I've even marked which ones."

"Anyway, dear, we really must clean and discard."

"OK, dear, if you insist."

The next morning Dusty was hard at work when his friend, J. W. Slickenside dropped by. "What are you doing, wearing your old khakis with paint on them, work shirt and even your clodhoppers on such a nice day?" he asked. "That doesn't look like fishing."

Dusty studied his shoes with steel caps on heel and toe. "I'm trying not to think about fishing today. See, JW, I sure couldn't get along without that wonderful wife of mine. But sometimes women are *so* particular. I figure we had lots of space left. Shouldn't really have to do this for another year, maybe longer with careful attention to stacking."

"Yup, Dusty, I have the same problem at home. Awful waste of time to clean the garage. But women do set a lot of store by tidiness. Tidiness for the *sake* of tidiness, I mean."

Dusty found a couple of wooden orchard apple boxes—the kind you don't often see anymore—carefully took fishing reels out of one and creels out of the other, transferred the equipment to empty cardboard cartons, and upended one for JW and another for himself. "See," he said, "A man needs a few empties around—gives flexibility. If I'd gotten rid of those cartons, we'd have no place to sit. Women just don't seem to understand such matters."

"Right you are, Dusty. By the way, what's in that crate?" He was referring to a wooden box the size of a washer and drier. The side that was in view was stencilled in big black characters:

電気発電機

(ガソリン使用)

"Just what it says, 'Electric Generator, Gasoline Powered.' It's Japanese."

"Really! I'm impressed! I didn't know you were a linguist."

"I don't brag about it. My vocabulary in that language is somewhat limited, but I figure that four

is a good start. I have a dictionary, and I've been intending to learn more."

"How did you come by the generator?"

"Well, it has quite a history. You know my old neighbor Jim? He was a Marine in World War II. They captured a lot of Japanese generators, and he brought one home. He gave it to me."

"Does it run?"

"Should be just fine. It's still in its original packing. He gave it to me in 1960. He'd never even unpacked it."

"Have you?"

"Nope."

"It sounds like something we could use on the farm. Are there instructions?"

"Sure, a whole book of them."

"Did you read them?"

"No, I haven't gotten around to it. That's why I got the dictionary, but I just haven't had time. I'll throw it in with the generator at no extra charge."

"With help like that, operating it shouldn't prove difficult. A Japanese exchange student is living next door to us this year. I'm sure he'd be glad to help."

"What's his major?"

"Medieval verse."

"Pretty handy with tools?"

"No, he's all thumbs, but don't worry. He'd only have to translate. I'd do the assembling. What do you want for it?"

Madge heard the end of this conversation as she came out to the garage. "We really should pay him to take it, Dusty."

"What about it, Dusty?" JW asked.

"Well, you know that portable electric fish smoker of yours?"

"Sure. My wife has been urging me to get rid of it. How about the fish smoker and five dollars?"

"Done!" said Dusty. "I'll help you load it into your pickup."

"Good. I'll bring over the fish smoker tomorrow afternoon."

JW opened his wallet and held out a five dollar bill. Just in time, too, for Dusty had his hand on his wallet, about to hold out his own.

After JW left, Dusty got right back to work. When Madge came at two p.m. he had three neatly labelled piles, GIVE AWAY which was small, KEEP which was large, and UNDECIDED, biggest of all.

"I thought JW took the generator," she said, looking at the familiar crate now in the middle of the garage floor.

"His wife said there wasn't room for it, so he paid me $5.00 to take it back. But he let me keep the fish smoker. See it there on the top shelf 'way at the back?"

He wagged his chin in the general direction of the shelves at the back of the garage. "That's funny," he said.

"What's funny?"

"It's that black box on the top shelf. I've never noticed it before. Wonder where it came from?" He stretched up and lifted down a box about the size of a small microwave oven.

It was of black wood, inlaid on sides, front, back and top with bits of shell in stylized designs. The top was the most ornate, with flower-like clusters, a pair of fighting cocks, and two like figures entwined in a circle, one red and the other of luminescent shell.

"Ebony!" said Madge. "Inlaid with polished shell and with a Yin and Yang symbol on the top. I've never seen an ebony box as large and as elaborate as this one. But Erma has a small one from Korea. This one also looks oriental, doesn't it?"

Now Erma, who disliked fish in any form, including living or dead, was not one of Dusty's favorite people. He just couldn't see why Madge enjoyed anyone so lacking in appreciation of the finer things in life.

"What does Erma know about it?" he asked with unwonted asperity. "Such fine craftsmanship must have been made in the U. S. of A."

He tried to open it. "Locked, by gum." He shook it. "Something inside. It sounds like paper rattling."

"It's lovely," Madge said, "but how did it get into our garage?"

"Must belong to the girls," Dusty said. "I'd better put it back where I found it."

But the girls knew nothing about it either. "Nope, Pop," Paula said. "Why don't you open it so we can see what's inside?"

By this time Dusty had found his old fly-tying outfit and was checking its contents. "Wow! There's even a Jungle Cock feather! You can't get those now the bird is an endangered species.

"I don't have time now, Pal. I'll get out my skeleton keys and open it this evening. Madge can have it to keep trinkets in. It'll look great on the sideboard in the dining room." He drew up a box to sit on and began to study the Jungle Cock feather.

Half an hour later, Madge came out to the garage accompanied by a heavy set man with dark hair and an expensive looking suntan. He was dressed in a handsome suit with white shirt and fat gold cufflinks. He was wearing dark glasses.

"Dusty, this is Mr. Smith-Jones. He's interested in that generator."

"Glad to meet you Mr. Smith-Jones. It's in that big box over there."

"Delighted to meet you, Mr. MacBugTussle. That generator is exactly what my employer needs, though I must say it is rather bigger than I'd expected. What would you take for it?"

"Well," Dusty said, "I guess five...., or....it's a popular item....maybe six...."

"Five thousand dollars! You drive a hard bargain. How about four, and we'll do the loading." He took out a roll of $100 bills and counted 40 of them into Dusty's trembling hand.

"Hey, Joe, Bill, bring the truck."

Two big men wearing blue jeans, black leather jackets and dark glasses picked up the generator and slid it into the truck. Smith-Jones got in on the passenger side, and off they drove.

"Gee," Dusty said.   "That generator's a real money maker. Wonder where we could get another one?

"Here," he said to Madge, "Would you please put this money in a safe place. We all can buy the things we've been wishing for, a trip to London for you, an Orvis rod for me, new bikes for the girls. We even can redecorate the living room, like we've been wanting to do."

"Oh, my! How nice! I do feel a little concerned that poor Mr. Smith-Jones may have paid too much for it, though of course, we can always refund the money if it doesn't work out for him. I was just on my way to the bank, so I'll deposit it into our savings account."

"Fine!" said Dusty, getting back to work.

Fifteen minutes later, when he was trying to decide whether to put the broken ski rack on the GIVE AWAY stack or on the UNDECIDED stack, two men with short haircuts and wearing grey slacks and brown jackets and looking like they meant business walked into the garage. They showed Dusty their FBI badges.

"Mr. MacBugTussle?" the taller of the two asked.

"That's me," Dusty said. "What can I do for you gentlemen?"

"We're looking for a Japanese box. We checked with your friend J.W. Slickenside, and he said he'd returned it to you. Something about not having enough room for it in his garage."

"*You* want to buy that box?   Gee, I'd like to oblige you, but a gentleman already got the only one I had, twenty minutes ago. I particularly noticed the time, because I wondered if I could just nip down to the creek and try my new fly rod before my wife returned from the bank. See, I want to be conscientious about this job, but..."

"Smith-Jones, eh? Heavy set, expensive clothes, dark glasses, two men with him named Bill and Joe. They wore blue jeans and leather jackets?"

"You got it exactly right. They must be friends of yours. I wish I could tell you where to find them, but they loaded up and drove off. Never a word about where they were going."

The FBI men looked around the garage. "Nothing left," the taller one said, handing Dusty a business card. "If you hear from them, Mr. MacBugTussle, let us know right away. This is our 24-hour number."

They'd barely gotten into their car when Smith-Jones came back. "I'm afraid this generator isn't what we thought, Mr. MacBugTussle. We'd like our money back."

"Gee, I'm sorry, but my wife was going to the bank; by now it's in our savings account. But we sure wouldn't want to cheat you. I'll phone the bank and see if I can catch her. Meanwhile, if you want you can unload the generator."

"Never mind the money," Smith-Jones said. "We're in a hurry. You don't have any other Japanese boxes, do you?"

"Nope, everything else was made in the good old USA."

"I thought not. Somebody gave us the wrong

information."

Just then several official vehicles pulled into the drive, and policemen and FBI agents got out. "Hands up, the lot of you," one of the agents said. "No, Mr. MacBugTussle, not you. We mean Smith-Jones and his helpers."

Suddenly everybody except Dusty was holding a gun and waving it at the others. Dusty tried to get out of the way, but Smith-Jones put an arm around his neck and hugged him close. "Let us go, or I'll shoot Mr. MacBugTussle," he said, edging out of the garage. The law men backed up and lowered their guns.

Then the screen door at the back of the house squeaked open and banged shut, and Madge called, "Dusty! Dusty! Telephone for you. It's Erma wanting to know about that ebony box on the shelf at the back of the garage. She's sure it came from Korea."

"Ebony box? Where is it?" Smith-Jones shouted and turned his head momentarily to look for it. "Grab it, Joe, and let's get out of here."

Dusty grabbed the gun, stomped on his captor's instep, ducked and heaved Smith-Jones over his shoulders to land him flat on his back on the concrete floor.

"Good for you, Dusty!" Madge said. "Excuse me, gentlemen, but I have a cake in the oven."

"And," said Dusty to Madge as he sat across the kitchen table watching her frost the cake, "Off they drove and they even let us keep the generator. I figure it's a great moneymaker; we certainly should put it in the KEEP pile."

"What about the ebony box, Dusty?   Did they take that?"

"No, the FBI man had a key that fit it.   He opened it and took out some papers. I said how much you liked the box, and he gave it to us. Said he'd like to have you on his side any day. Said he thought you deserved a reward. He even left the key for you."

THE DUMPSTER

"I see that the dumpster has come, Dusty," Madge MacBugTussle said as they were doing the breakfast dishes.

"Where is it, anyway? I asked them to put it beside the garage, but it sure isn't there."

"There are two of them alongside the main road."

"*Two* of 'em! I ordered one. They can just come and get the extra. I ordered one, and I'll pay for one. And that's that!"

"Oh, it's all right, dear. Our new neighbors got the second one."

"New neighbors! What new neighbors?"

"The people who bought the old Smith place. Their name is Frillingbee, John and Edith. I met them out front yesterday when I was picking up the *Press Democrat*. They seem quite personable. She's a mechanical engineer, and he's a pastry cook. They have two boys and a girl, all in university."

"Wow! Three kids in college! I thought two was a lot. They sure don't need a dumpster. How could they possibly afford to throw anything away?"

He hung the dishtowel on the rack above the stove and picked up his cap. "I think I'll mosey on down and check things out," he said.

There were two big dumpsters parked end-to-end

beside the road. A brawny middle aged man with thinning blond hair and red face was looking them over when Dusty arrived. "Hello," he said. "You must be Dusty MacBugTussle; I'm John Frillingbee."

"Right! Glad to meet you."

The two shook hands then circled the dumpsters warily, demarcating the boundaries of their territories.

"I'll tell my family to use the blue one," Frillingbee said. "The red one is for you."

"What do you mean?" Dusty said. "The red one is beside your driveway and the blue one beside ours. Anybody could see that the blue one is for us."

The two were standing with arms akimbo staring at each other when the paper boy came by. "Hi there!" he said. "Whatcha looking at?"

"These dumpsters," Frillingbee said. "We're deciding who gets which."

"Why don't you just flip a coin? Here, I have a nickel. Heads it's your choice; tails it's Mr. MacBugTussle's." He flipped the coin. "Heads it is," he said.

"I'll take the blue one," Frillingbee said.

"It's going to be pretty inconvenient for you to carry stuff around the red one to put it in the blue," the boy pointed out.

Frillingbee looked surprised. "You have a good point, young man. I choose the red one. And I'm not going to change my mind whatever *you* say, MacBugTussle."

The boy bicycled off, and the two men marched up their driveways without further conversation.

"The children wanted sack lunches, so it's just the two of us," Madge said. "Will you do the salad?"

"Well, I met Frillingbee," Dusty said, cutting a tomato. "He's kind of hard-headed, but he can be persuaded by reason."

"Yes, I think we'll enjoy having them next door," Madge said.

She picked up a pot holder and took the rolls out of the oven. "I've been wondering. Do you think there will be space in the dumpster for those things I found in the attic? There's that old TV set, the bicycle with only one wheel, and a lot of broken lawn furniture."

"Sure. I also plan to put in all that stuff from the garage. We haven't had anyone asking to buy that Japanese generator recently. I think I'll put it in, too."

"Good idea," she agreed.

Suddenly they heard sirens. "Another fire engine, I suppose," said Dusty.

The phone rang. Dusty answered. When he came back, he had his hat in his hand. "I guess I'll put my food in the oven. Somebody robbed the Slickensides just a few minutes ago, and JW wants me to help hunt for him. Can you believe it? In broad daylight with the people at home.

"He took the sterling silver tea set, a tape recorder, some jewelry, and not only that but JW's entire supply of Lady Jane Hanigan dry flies, his best Orvis reel, and who knows what else. JW surprised the thief stuffing things into a pillowcase. The man ran out to the street with JW hot on his heels. Then he simply disappeared."

"Barely a block away! I wonder if the thief has come this way? Oh, Dusty, do be careful!"

Dusty helped search for an hour, but the thief was nowhere to be seen—not in the garage, not in the house, not out back in the woodshed, not anywhere. He'd vanished as if he'd never been there.

The police took statements from the Slickensides, from Dusty (which only shows how desperate they were, for his information was entirely hearsay), and from a little old gentleman who'd been walking down the street. No leads! They got into their squad cars, turned off the sirens, and went back to the station.

Dusty'd barely returned to the house when his youngest daughter, Paula, came running up the drive. "Pop! Pop!" she cried. "Bring a ladder!"

"What's wrong, Pal? Kite up a tree again?"

But it wasn't a kite this time. She and her little friend, Buster, had been playing hide and seek. The dumpster was a wonderful hiding place, and it had taken her an hour and a half to find him. Now he was very tired of it, but it was too deep for him to escape.

"Hurry!" she urged. "Buster wants to get out of the blue dumpster, and so does that little man in the red one. Please hurry!"

Dusty called 9-1-1, got the ladder and went down to the road. He rescued Buster, who thanked him profusely, then turned to the other dumpster, where a small man in blue jeans and work shirt sat on the floor with a bulging pillow case beside him.

"I'm Dusty MacBugTussle," he said.

"Pleased to meet you. People call me Mickey."

"Why didn't you climb out?" Dusty asked.

"What, and leave the loot? It's too heavy for me to climb out with it. Think of it, mister. Get myself out and sacrifice this treasure? Do you know there's a whole box of Lady Jane Hanigan flies? A new Orvis reel—I've been wanting one for years—and a silver tea set. Nope! People say you can't take it with you. But I'll stick to my possessions as long as I can."

Dusty thought that there was something commendable in his decision, especially about the reel and the flies. Clearly Mickey was no common run of the mill thief.

Dusty would have liked to put the ladder down and let things take their own course. It was only because he was a super law-abiding citizen who already had called the police that he restrained himself.

"Don't worry, mister, I've been there before." Mickey said, noticing Dusty's doleful face. "Can't beat jail for free room and board. Comfortable cell, though somewhat small, warm, plenty of food, though the menu is a bit repetitious. Friends all around me; even the guards call me by my first name. I'll be OK."

A few minutes later Mickey, still clutching his pillowcase, waved goodbye from the rear seat of the police cruiser.

"Now there," said Dusty, "Is a man who has his priorities straight."

The next morning Dusty loaded the wheelbarrow with stuff from the DISCARD pile in the garage and wheeled it down to the blue dumpster. Somebody had already been filling the red one. He glanced over the side and saw the parts to an ancient walk-in ice box. The Frillingbees were cleaning the barn.

By lunch time, there were big piles of stuff in both of the dumpsters. "By golly," Dusty said to Madge, "I sure hate to see them throw away old Smith's nets, rods, and lures. But they're discarding the lot."

"Well, Dusty, they probably aren't fishermen, and there's plenty of junk in that barn. You've said that yourself."

"Yup, but it's *good* old junk. A fellow could do a lot with it."

By mid afternoon, Dusty was ready to quit. "I'll finish tomorrow," he said to Madge as he quaffed the glass of lemonade she brought out to the garage where he was sitting on an upturned box. "I'm just going down to take one more look before I call it a day."

He looked into the blue dumpster, impressed at the progress he'd made. Then he looked into the red one. By golly, old Smith's surf net was right on top of the load. Nobody was in sight, so he climbed in. It would only take him a moment to throw the net into his own dumpster, where he could rescue it at his leisure.

Once inside, he could see other stuff that he really wanted. He tossed the surf net, followed it with a couple of poke poles, and a crab net. There was that old box of lures.

He just was getting nicely into the rhythm of the tossing, when he noticed a ski rack in the dumpster beside him. Hmmmnnn, that sure looked familiar. So did the old TV set and the bicycle with only one wheel that were beside it.

It was when he tossed the big landing net that he decided something was really fishy, for it collided in mid air with a lawn chair that looked very much like the one he'd put in his dumpster just that morning. And he barely ducked in time when an old cast iron frying pan sailed over clearing his head by inches.

"Hey, you, watch where you're throwing things. You almost hit me." He jumped to his feet and scrambled out of the dumpster.

A willowy middle aged blond with blue eyes and plenty of laugh lines on her face popped up from the blue dumpster. "Dusty!" she said.

"Why it's Edith Simpson," he said. "Haven't seen you since we went to the Senior Prom together."

"Edith Simpson Frillingbee," she corrected. "My, we had a good time, didn't we!

"But down to business. I thought I could use a few of the things from your dumpster. I was just tossing them into ours till I have time to take them home."

"Me, too," he said. "Just some old fishing equipment that I thought I might use sometime."

"There's lots more fishing equipment up in our barn," she said. "Bring your wheelbarrow, and take what you can use. No sense in my carrying it down and you carrying it back–though I have to admit that the game of exchanging was amusing while it lasted. Just like the fishpond at the PTA Carnival."

"Take whatever you wish," Dusty said. "Is there anything I can help you with?"

"Why yes," she said. "There's an old generator in that big wooden box. I'd love to rebuild it for our mountain cabin."

"No problem at all," said Dusty. "I'll get my come-along winch and have it out in no time."

After dinner, when he and Madge were sitting in front of the fire, Dusty told her about the fine culch he'd gotten and given. "It's a shame we rented two dumpsters," he said. "What with exchanging so much stuff, both of us together won't fill one."

"Waste not; want not," Madge said. "I'm glad you and Edith are such practical people. John Frillingbee may be a bit inflexible, but all in all, I think we'll enjoy our new neighbors."

DUSTY MACBUGTUSSLE
AND THE HUMAN GENOME

Dusty MacBugTussle was sprawled on the warm sand, a coffee cup in one hand and a cheese on rye sandwich in the other, basking in the sun's rays, enjoying the salt spray mist and idly watching several Surf Scoters swimming through the breakers. Only his fisherman's sixth sense was attuned to the surf rod sticking up beside him in its holder. All the rest of his senses could be said to be on holiday, idling languidly along in neutral as he contemplated the meaning of life and why it is best to be a fisherman.

He knew that if he stood up he could see fishing boats out beyond the breakers even as far away as the horizon. And if he walked to the top of the dune behind him, he could see boats still farther away. It was nice to know this and not have to do it.

He put the cup and the sandwich on top of the picnic hamper, lounged to his feet and took the rod out of its holder. He pulled back on it to lift the bait off the bottom, set the rod butt against his stomach, and reeled in.

"Hmmmnnn," he muttered, "Bait's gone." He reached into a bucket, took out a piece of fish gut, threaded it onto the hook, swung the rod tip back, and cast out beyond the first line of breakers with a deceptively effortless motion, the result of years of practice. "That's the spot," he said, set the rod in its holder, and relaxed back onto the sand.

He fingered the goose egg above his ear, incurred when he came up suddenly—much too suddenly—under the open cupboard door as he was loading the dishwasher this morning. It hadn't, he reflected, seemed a felicitous event when it happened, but only time tells with such occurrences. And who wouldn't endure a few moments of pain in exchange for an afternoon of surf casting?

His dear wife, Madge, had not only understood his need for quiet and fresh air after the accident, she had insisted on packing a lunch while he assembled his fishing gear. So here he was drinking in the sunshine with only enough action from the fish to keep him from falling asleep.

If he weren't here, he'd be home spading the flower beds and mowing the lawns. A slight guilt feeling nibbled at his conscience, but he quieted it by telling himself, "There is a time and a season for everything under the sun." And a man certainly couldn't fault the sun that was right here on Salmon Creek Beach today.

The rod tip twitched—once—twice—and then the line began to run out and the reel to whir. He abandoned philosophy, jumped to his feet, grabbed the rod and set the hook. Suddenly he was the wide awake fisherman known throughout the west for his incredible catches.

"Onto a big one," he said, letting the fish run.

He was still masterfully managing the monster, reeling in slack when he could, letting it run when he had to, when two men approached and stood watching him.

They were dressed in clothing more appropriate to corporate offices or bank headquarters than to the beach. Both wore white shirts with ties, black suits with razor sharp creases, and now-dusty patent leather shoes. The first man carried nothing, while the one who followed wore a white lab coat over his suit, carried a second lab coat over one arm and lugged, really almost dragged, an enormous briefcase with the other.

The two watched MacBugTussle race up the beach to slide in a huge ling cod. "Bravo! Bravo! Bravissimo!" they shouted, jumping up and down and clapping their hands as Dusty clubbed the flailing fish.

The leader leaned over the fish, "Three feet long if it's an inch," he judged. "What an amazing catch! I wouldn't believe it if I hadn't seen it happen."

"Hmmmnnn," Dusty observed. "Not bad for an afternoon trip."

But even the unflappable fisherman momentarily appeared surprised when he looked more closely at the newcomers. He could see that their attire was different from his own blue work shirt, old shoes, hooded sweatshirt and khaki pants with a red patch that his youngest daughter had sewed over a hole in the knee. All he said, however, was "I see you've got your creel. What kind of fish are you after?"

"Not fish, my dear Mr. MacBugTussle," the leader replied, "for surely I am standing face-to-face with *the* Dusty MacBugTussle, known worldwide for his brilliant pursuit of the finny tribe. We come not as anglers but to study anglers, to prostrate ourselves at the feet of the legendary angler."

He dug through the briefcase and brought out a richly engraved business card,

---

G. Wesley Whifflebar, PhD, Scientist, Phrenologist.

Senior Partner, Whifflebar, Whifflebar & Whifflebar.

We Map The Human Genome. Fishermen Our Specialty.

"I am Dr. Whifflebar, and this gentleman is P.R. Pollypop, my assistant. Perhaps you've heard, Mr. MacBugTussle, about the huge project to map the human genome?"

"Can't say I have," Dusty replied. "What kind of fish is it?"

"Not exactly a fish. The human genome is the arrangement of the genes that determines hereditary traits. The job of mapping what trait is on what gene has been divided up among many labs."

"I see. And your business?"

"Is to study the part of the genome that determines fishermen's interests and skills.

"We're into DNA and RNA," Whifflebar said modestly. "We've found that fishing success underlies all success, Mr. MacBugTussle. Our firm has qualified for a megabuck federal grant. We're mapping the fisherman genetic code."

"Yup," Dusty observed, "I've always maintained it's merely a case of presenting the right bait to the right fish. The concept underlies our entire free enterprise, capitalistic system. Now take this ling cod, for example..."

"You're absolutely right," Whifflebar said, putting out his arms as Pollypop helped him into his handsome lab coat with a tastefully twined "WW" monogram on the pocket. "This study will move Phrenology a quantum leap forward. We'll publish a research article in *Science* within a month and a major article within six months. Our findings will be the hottest subject to hit the newsstands in this decade."

Pollypop, perspiring vigorously, opened the collar of his lab coat. "Yes, Pollypop, go right ahead. It's all right for young people to disrobe at the beach. I encourage informality in all my assistants."

"Very good, Dr. Whifflebar," said Pollypop taking off his lab coat, then his coat, and even rolling up his shirtsleeves.

"Do sit down!" said Whifflebar, pressing Dusty's shoulders and moving the bait bucket behind him. He reached up to run his hand over MacBugTussle's head. "The science of Phrenology is served by a hands-on approach to the skull."

"If you'll just excuse me a moment, I'll bait up and get back to fishin'," Dusty apologized, neatly sidestepping the bait bucket. "Don't want to waste fishin' time." He baited up, cast again, and sat down on the picnic hamper.

"Make yourselves at home," he invited. "Either

one of you care for a cup of coffee or a cheese on rye? My wife makes the *best* sandwiches."

"I'm sure she does, Mr. MacBugTussle, but we've just had lunch. Thanks anyway."

Whifflebar knelt on the sand beside Dusty and held out his hand for a pair of calipers. Pollypop gave them to him then took up a clipboard and poised a pencil ready to record Whifflebar's every word.

"Now look first at the size and general shape of the skull," Whifflebar instructed Pollypop, running his hand over Dusty's head. "Ah! *Large* with plenty of cranial capacity, truly a brainy individual. *Square* with the stubborn streak that underlies unswerving pursuit of his prey. *Smooth* which permits thoughts to circulate freely within his brain."   He made several measurements.

"*Now!* This magnificent knowledge bump above his right ear is the most significant single indication of Mr. MacBugTussle's hereditary predisposition to piscatorial prowess. (Remind me, Pollypop, to show you my monograph on the subject.)   Just as I hypothesized, a right brain dominant fisherman. Right brain creativity-that's the key to it. You see, there is so much brain power within the cranium at this point that the skull has bulged to accommodate it."

"Take it easy on that bump," Dusty said. "It's sore as a boil."

"Yes," said Whifflebar, "Yes, here it is, though I'll need to modify my hypothesis slightly as to the physiognomical position of the feature. But all in all, it's a breakthrough for the study of the fishing gene."

Dusty wiped his hand over his head and brushed off the calipers. Whifflebar reluctantly concluded this part of his examination and took an expensive looking camera.

"Now, just hold the pole." He instructed Dusty. "Look at the fish. Ahh! Perfect! Don't move. Excellent! Now turn your head to show the knowledge bump-very pronounced in your case, Mr. MacBugTussle just as we'd expect of a world class fisherman like you. Right brain! Creative! A classic example!

"Just think of the commercial possibilities," he said to Pollypop. "This day has furthered our line of discovery by years. With gene splicing we can create a master race of corporate executives. We'll rule the world."

Pollypop cleared his throat, "erm...erm...If I could offer a suggestion, sir...?"

"Certainly. I welcome suggestions."

"Well, sir, most corporate executives are 'Type A personalities.' I wonder....?" He wagged his chin toward MacBugTussle who was reclining on the sand with one eye barely open enough to see the fishing rod.

"Hmmmn, yes, I see what you mean, Pollypop. It'll be all right, though. Perhaps we'll splice genes from several sources to get the desired attributes. We'll use MacBugTussle for fishing expertise, me for ability to work under high pressure, as on this beach, and you for alertness in adversity. If we manage well, you should be able to capitalize on your contributions to the study.

"Yes, Pollypop, I can see you now, Dr. Percival

Pollypop, in your monogrammed lab coat, your microscope, computer and calipers on your executive desk, holding your solid gold pencil in your hand. You'll enjoy all the perquisites of exemplary achievement, all the plaudits of a grateful world, just like me. Yes, the procedure'll just need a little fine-tuning.

"And now, if you'll take the camera, you might just get a picture of Mr. MacBugTussle and me. Wait till I get the calipers. A photo does increase the newsworthiness of the story. It's only prudent to anticipate the needs of the press."

Pollypop took several shots. "That should do it, sir."

Whifflebar dusted off his hands then turned to Dusty. "Let's keep this plan between ourselves, Mr. MacBugTussle. We'll be getting in touch with you as soon as details can be worked out. This will be the gene-splicing coup of the year. We'll borrow one of your fishing genes—a totally harmless and painless process—and inject it into bacteria then insert the bacteria into a human being, transferring the gene to people who lack your quality. It'll make your fortune, Mr. MacBugTussle, mark my words. Your fortune and the fortune of Whifflebar, Whifflebar, and Whifflebar, Scientists."

"There's just one thing I want to point out," Dusty said when Whifflebar paused for breath. "About this expensive piece of fine craftsmanship which you are calling a 'pole.' My dear wife and little daughters gave it to me for my last birthday. Notice the fine finish, the graduated guides, the reel for the line. This is called a 'fishing rod.' A 'fishing pole,' on the other hand, has the line attached to the end of the pole. If you're gonna be around fish, you need to get that right."

"Yes, well, thank you, Mr. MacBugTussle. So nice of you to set me straight. We'll be getting in touch with you soon about that other matter. Now remember! Mum's the word." He gave Dusty a hearty handshake, handed his lab coat to Pollypop, and led the way as the two slogged off across the sand.

That evening while Dusty was preparing to bake the fish, Madge MacBugTussle put her hand on the bump on his head. "If that isn't better by tomorrow, dear, I think you should see the doctor."

"Oh, it's OK, dear. There was a little guy at the beach this afternoon, a doctor somebody. He examined it closely. Seemed quite pleased with it in fact.

"I'm not sure why he came to the beach, though. All dressed up like a card shark and couldn't tell a rod from a pole. Must not be much of a fisherman."

THE HOUSE SITTERS

Though events chronicled below are fabricated, abalone poaching is a real threat to coastal wildlife. In December, 1991, for example, two men were caught at Fort Ross with 161 abalone. In August 1993, authorities arrested another man believed to be the ringleader of a band of over twenty shellfish poachers. He had in his boat a secret compartment where abalone were concealed. He also was accused of taking 1,000 pounds of sea urchins at Salt Point State Park, a closed area.

At-the-Bay
January 26, 1993

Dear Grandpop,
Hope you and JW are enjoying the conference. We saw an article about it in the *New York Times*. It said that the piscatorial illiteracy of American school children is a national disgrace. They are shockingly deficient compared with the average child in Japan, Britain, or even Burkina Faso. More than 80% of them can't tell a trout from a shark. But there's new hope. Your Flycasters' Conference is spearheading a program to require a fish pond in every home. Clio and I say *Bravo!*
We had a card from Mother. She says London

is wonderful beyond even her fondest imaginings. Grandmother said to remind you to wear your hat and gloves.

Clio and I went to the marina to check on the boats. JW's dory is taking water and needs to be pumped. Your dinghy is OK, and the big boat is fine, but we were surprised to find dirty dishes in the sink and no food in the refrigerator. You must have left in a hurry. We spruced everything up and will get some stuff to re-stock the freezer tomorrow when we shop for groceries.

Tell JW that his cats are fine and so is his philodendron.

Love, Thalia

At-The-Conference
February 4, 1993

Dear Girls,

I'm glad the folks are having a good time in London. They certainly mustn't miss the boat museum at Greenwich.

There are lots of retailers here crowding around to order the Lady Jane Hanigan fly, so it was well worthwhile to come. But I haven't had a rod and reel in my hand since I arrived. No fishing; not even a pond around; just meetings. Depressing!

JW and I talked over the boat situation. We tried to phone you, but no one answered. He thinks that something fishy is going on at the marina, and you girls should not get near it. Don't worry about his dory; it has taken in rainwater and will have to be bailed—no need to bother till he gets back.

We have decided to take the optional field trip, but we'll be home in a week.

Love, Grandpop

At-The-Bay
February 8, 1993

Dear Grandpop,
Today it's my turn to write a letter and Thalia's to feed the cats and water the philodendron.

JW's dory is on the bottom. It was sinking when we got to the harbor yesterday. The drain plug was gone, and we couldn't find one that would fit. We bailed as fast as we could, but it sank anyway. The water is so murky we can't actually see the boat, but fortunately the mooring buoy is still afloat, so we won't have any problem finding it.

When we got to your boat this afternoon there were two big rough looking men standing on the deck. They were in their late twenties, tall and blond with lots of long hair. They both were wearing wetsuits. They said their names were Joe and Bill, and that they were fishing friends of yours. They knew you were at the conference and mentioned the Lady Jane Hanigan fly.

We wonder if they're the people who ate up the supplies and left the dirty dishes. We pretended to believe them, but we found a phone booth and called the Deputy Sheriff. By the time he came they'd gone.

The mail is slow. The only thing that's come from you is a letter that you sent on February 4th. We're glad you are receiving lots of orders, and we hope you are getting out and having a good time.

Tell JW his cats and his philodendron are fine. His prize tomcat, Smokey, sure eats a lot.

Love, Clio

At-the-Conference
February 10, 1993

Dear Girls,

We've tried several times to call you, but the operator says your phone is out of order.

Don't worry about the boats. Stay away from the marina.   JW says there are some pretty tough characters who could be a heap of trouble. *Stay away from the marina*; when JW and I get home, we'll take care of things. Meanwhile, don't go near the marina.

We've decided not to stay for the field trip.

Love, Grandpop

At-The-Bay
February 8, 1993

Dear Grandpop,

It's my turn to write today. Clio is feeding the cats and watering the philodendron.

The cabin in your boat really stank yesterday,

and when we put the garbage out, we found abalone guts in it. Clio and I think Bill and Joe are abalone poachers. What's more, they seem to be using your boat for their headquarters. We think those ruffians were counting on you being out of town and were surprised to see us.

We reported our suspicions to the game warden, but he says he'd need evidence before he could take any action. By the time he'd get here, the men and the evidence would be gone. Clio and I think kids are better than adults at sleuthing, because we *look* innocent, and we don't fiddle around with a lot of silly rules.

Tell JW that Smoky gets fatter every day. Other than that, the cats look fine. So does the philodendron.

Love, Thalia

At-The-Bay
February 11, 1993

Dear Grandpop,
Wow! Thalia finally got her scuba gear yesterday. It's just what we need to raise JW's dory! Full speed ahead!

This morning we found a drain plug and got a few inner tubes to fasten to the thwarts. We planned to pump them up to raise it then put in the plug and bail the water out.

We fit everything into your dinghy, rowed out and dropped anchor ten feet from the buoy that marks the dory. We brought fishing equipment for cover just in case anyone was watching.

Everything started out as planned. Thalia took first turn, since it's her scuba gear. I began casting an anchovy with my old spinning outfit.

Then! What a surprise! She'd no sooner gone down than those ruffians arrived in a little inflatable boat. Bill was wearing a wet suit.

They rowed over toward us, and Joe shouted, "Hey you! Where's your girl friend? Did she fall out of the boat?" They laughed so hard I thought one of them would fall overboard.

"Can't you see I'm busy?" I replied frostily. "Don't get any closer; you'll scare the fish!" But I could see they intended to come right on over. What to do? Obviously extreme measures were necessary.

I took out that old catch-all lure with the four sets of triple hooks. You know the one that snags anything it comes in contact with. I checked wind direction, flexed my arm a few times, and made a perfect cast. The lure fell into the bottom of their boat about half way between the two. I twitched the rod tip to jerk the hook—or hooks, as the case may be—into the gunwale then pulled hard to break the line and leave the lure as a reminder. "Do be careful!" I said. "I might snag *you* if you get too close."

"Dumb sport fishermen!" Joe shouted, "always messing around in the harbor and interfering with honest people like me." But they moved away and dropped anchor two hundred feet from us. Bill slipped over the gunwale and into the water. He swam a few strokes toward the dory and dived.

Well! I didn't have any way of warning Thalia they were there, so I just kept on pretending I was fishing and hoped for the best.

When Thalia came up, I motioned her to stay on the off side of our boat so they couldn't see her. "Forget raising the dory," she said. "There's more important work to do. Somebody's got sacks of abalone in it. They're poachers like we've been reading about in the paper!"

I barely had time to tell her that "somebody" was Bill and Joe when Bill surfaced on the near side of our boat. "Dammit, Joe," he said. "The water's so murky I can't find the dory."

"I'm not Joe," I said. "Bug off."

But the next time he came up beside us again. He'd dived repeatedly but still hadn't found the boat. In fact, he seemed to have trouble finding anything. Apparently it didn't occur to him to follow the line that was attached to the buoy. He's a real sleaze. Thalia said he'd been drinking.

A few minutes later, he and Thalia surfaced simultaneously. I leaned over with my back toward him to ask her if she wanted to quit. Suddenly he was trying to climb into our boat.

"Get out of here!" I said, and gave him a push. Unfortunately I was off balance; he grabbed my arm, and I fell into the water on top of him.

Thalia realized something was wrong and came around and shoved him away from me. In the general confusion Bill didn't realize he was dealing with two people. "Peace! Peace!" he said, and swam off toward where Joe was.

As I climbed back aboard, I finally had a chance to talk with Thalia. "What can we do? By the time we can notify the game warden, they'll be long gone."

"I know!" she said and dived again.

After he'd dived half a dozen times, Bill shouted, "Hey! A sea lion grabbed me. It bumped into me and grabbed me."

"You're imagining things," Joe said.

"No, it kept bumping against me, and it grabbed my arm. See, the sleeve is torn."

That got me worried. What if the sea lion grabbed Thalia?

"Quit your stalling. We've been here half an hour. All you need to do is check the abs. Get going."

Bill dived again. When he came up he said, "I found the dory, but that sea lion must be after our catch. It keeps poking around. The water's so murky I can hardly see my hand in front of my face. It's scary down there."

"Sea lion hunh!" Joe said. "Cut it out. We need to deliver 'em tomorrow morning. Just check the sacks and be sure everything is OK. Quit making excuses and get with it."

"OK, here I go, but this is my last dive, see!" He was down a very short time, and when he surfaced, his "All OK" seemed too pat to me, but Joe helped him aboard, weighed anchor, and rowed toward the marina.

Where was Thalia? Surely she'd fight if the sea lion grabbed her.

Mustn't blow our cover, though. I stood up and cast, then reeled in slowly. Unfortunately a silly mackerel grabbed the bait, and I was busy playing a fish when actually I wanted to find her and get out of there. I finally got it up to the boat and released it.

I was just preparing to cast again when there was a quiet slurping sound as Thalia came up. "I did it," she said. "Let's get back to the marina." I helped her into the boat and rowed home.

"Who'd ever think" she said, "of looking there for abalone? I fooled them, though. I took one sack and tied it to the pilings that support the channel marker."

That Thalia! She has some great ideas.

"What about the sea lion? Did it bother you?"

"Sea lion? Did Bill say that? The water's so murky I just kept bumping into him, but, of course, he wouldn't know it was me."

Of course, we were elated at our good fortune in being on the scene of the crime. Talk about evidence; we had it! But there's never a game warden around when you need one. The poachers left the marina before we even got a dial tone, so we hung up. The heck with game wardens. We decided to catch the crooks ourselves.

Love, Clio

P.S. Tell JW that Smokey doesn't seem to be sick, but he keeps hiding in the broom closet. We just can't think what possesses that cat. The other cats and the philodendron are fine.

At-The-Conference
February 11, 1993

Telegram

Girls Stop Do not go near the marina Stop Stay out of the boats Stop Do not go near the harbor Stop Phone me when you get this Stop.

Love, Grandpop

At-the-Bay
February 12, 1993

Dear Grandpop,

Don't worry. the mailman delivered all your messages this afternoon. We'd already solved the problem. The poachers are in jail.

Bill and Joe both dived this morning. Of course, each of them thought the other had taken that sack that Thalia moved. They shouted so loud we could even hear them from the shore. Then they got into a big fistfight right there in the water. For awhile we worried that one of them might drown, the way they were punching, kicking and biting.

As soon as we saw that they were fully occupied, we called the game warden. He brought the Deputy Sheriff and two men in wet suits. It wasn't hard to catch the poachers; they had tired each other out.

For awhile as things were developing, I was worried that the sack we moved might lead to our being accused of aiding the poachers. But Thalia solved that problem. Once Bill and Joe were fighting and before the game warden came, she dived down and put the hidden sack back with the others.

It was a thoroughly satisfying outcome. The game warden said it's the biggest bust yet. He shook hands with Thalia and me and said he'll recommend us for a medal.

What an adventure! We wouldn't have missed it for the world.

When all the excitement was over, we put the drain plug into the dory, floated it, and pumped it out, just as we'd planned. It was a bit muddy, but we scrubbed it with the vegetable brush from the kitchen sink.

Things here are pretty slow. We're staying away from the marina, just as you said. Some big boxes have floated in on the ocean beach, and JW's neighbor says the Coast Guard was closing in on some dope smugglers who jettisoned their cargo to avoid arrest. We'll go out this afternoon to see for ourselves.

Love, Clio.

P.S. Thalia is feeding the cats. I watered the philodendron. We plan to spend more time playing with Smokey and the kittens, get them accustomed to people. They're beautiful! We know JW will be delighted to have six cats when he gets home instead of the three he left.

REPORT FROM THE LAKE

Dear reader, at our lake there are many boulders, each one special to its friends. Rest assured that the one in this story is your Big Blue Boulder.

Dusty MacBugTussle was enjoying the warmth of the morning sun on his back. He was sitting on the boulder behind his cabin using his best tinsnips and carefully cutting along lines he'd drawn on a shiny tomato can, which he was preparing to make into a spinner. Hearing the crunching sound of footsteps in decomposed granite, he looked up. There was his friend, J.W. Slickenside, striding down the hill.

"Hello, Hello, Dusty," Slickenside said. "What are you doing sitting there on that glacial erratic?" He gave the boulder a good whack with his rock hammer.

An unseating rumble sent Dusty scrambling to his feet, and a deep, rusty voice said, "Whaddaya mean, 'erratic'? I'm the most stable rock on this side of the lake. And stop pounding on my sore hip."

"Whoops!" Dusty said, catching his balance. "That rock can talk."

"Of course I can talk," said Big Blue Boulder. "What do you think I am, dumb?"

"Of course not, not dumb but surely silent," replied Dusty. "In fact, I've lived here more than sixty years and I've never heard a peep out of you before."

"Well, nobody called me erratic before. If I'm erratic, he's capricious, here today and gone tomorrow like an insect. In fact, where did he come from? I've never set eyes on him before in all my life."

Big Blue shifted slightly, and dust flew from under him. Slickenside and MacBugTussle jumped back in alarm.

"I apologize! Hold it! I'm sorry I whacked you, and please! Don't get me wrong," Slickenside cried. "I was only describing you in geologist's terms. A 'glacial erratic' is a boulder that differs from the other rock in its immediate vicinity, one that has been moved from elsewhere by a glacier. I bet it was an eye opening experience."

"Wow! It was," said Big Blue, mollified by the sincerity of the apology. "I'd resided for aeons among my own kind deep in the wilderness. It was pleasant but dull. I'd always longed to travel but never had the opportunity. Then along came a glacier—Louis was his name, Louis Agassiz—a huge body of moving ice that swept up everybody in his path. You can't imagine; he was like dozens of freight trains.

"I struck up acquaintance with a few boulders that already were on board, and they encouraged me. So I contracted with a squirrel to tunnel under my left shoulder, shook a little to give gravity a chance, and rolled down onto the ice."

"Wow!   Riding on a glacier," Slickenside exclaimed. "I've seen rocks polished slick as a whistle by the sandpaperlike action of the ice—glacial polish

they call it. And gouges. And roche moutonnée, and lots of moraines. But tell me about riding on a glacier. What an adventure."

"It was the giddiest experience of my life. We rushed for miles at a breathtaking speed of inches a day. Finally Louis stopped moving and melted down and gradually left me among these strangers."

"Yes," MacBugTussle said. "I can see that you're different from the rocks around you. Prettier, too. How do you get along with them?"

"Well, thank you," Big Blue said, "I am obviously of a superior strain, the very upper crust of rocks in the Sierra. My new neighbors immediately recognized my worth and made me their leader. Since then we've gotten along cordially for aeons and aeons.

"I'm very stable and dependable. You might think of me as Lord of the Manor; I attend all the parties, award prizes at competitions, and give an annual End-of-Season celebration for the surrounding countryside. All the boulders and their pebbles come dressed in their best. Games, food, music (hard rock, of course), it's a real gala. Yes, I wouldn't move now; I'm quite content."

"Well, Big Blue, I'm honored to have my cabin near such a distinguished leader." Dusty said. "I'll......"

"Owh! Oogh! It's my sciatica again!"

"Oh, you poor boulder," MacBugTussle exclaimed. "I can *see* the crack. How long has it being going on?"

"Only a few hundred years, really, but it seems like ages. It's so painful I don't dare move around."

"Can't anything be done for you?" Slickenside asked.

"I really need an injection of quartz. That would cure it right up."

"Yes," said MacBugTussle, "I've noticed bands of quartz in rock. It pushes in and fills breaks, sort of glues the rock together again."

"Well, the treatment does work on buried rocks, but so far the Regolith Health Service won't pay for it on surface individuals like me. Even the FDA won't approve it for general use. They say it's experimental."

"No chance of getting it on the fast track? Declaring it a matter of life or death?"

"Aeons away!"

"What about going underground?"

"I've thought of it, I tell you. But if I did I'd start out again on the lowest rung of the ladder of success, go wherever the authorities sent me. There's a lot of jealousy. I'd be at the mercy of some minor clerk in the personnel department. That doesn't appeal to a long-established boulder like me.

"I can understand your concern; it would be risky," MacBugTussle said thoughtfully.

"Who knows! I might be dragged under a continental plate," Big Blue continued. "Or I'd lose my identity, in the lava of one of those Hawaiian volcanoes. The eruptions on the Big Island are always seeking volunteers; next thing they'll institute the draft. No! I'll take my chances right here where I'm well known."

"I see your point," said Slickenside. "It would be

hard to give up this sylvan Sierra scene just to be melted and assigned somewhere else."

"Right! There are some situations worse than sciatica." Big Blue said. "But speaking of dire situations, what's this I heard about sedimentary rocks rolling from the ridge and headed in this direction?"

"That's what I came to observe," Slickenside said. "That's why I wore my field clothing, boots, shirt, cap, rock hammer. Have any of them gotten this far?"

"Not yet, but I'm worried. *Our* community—all I've worked for—is at stake. We're all Igneous Rocks in this neighborhood. We don't want any of those Sedimentaries moving in."

"You sound like you've had a bad experience," Slickenside observed.

"I'll say! It was back in my old neighborhood. The Creamy Cliff Limestone family moved in; their homestead was a disgrace, with little white chips everywhere. Property prices plummeted. The neighborhood beautification committee tried everything, but they wouldn't clean up their place."

"Whatever did you do?" Dusty asked.

"The situation was desperate. We called in Ebenezer Erosion—you've probably seen his bulldozers around with the motto WE MOVE MOUNTAINS in big white letters. He got right at the Limestones and reduced them to shards."

"Then what?"

"Oh, when the lot of them were shards and weathered, he flowed 'em out of town in a rill."

"Don't you mean, 'rode 'em out on a rail?'

Dusty asked.

"You humans! Always tinkering with history. Why don't you listen when a boulder speaks?"

"You were lucky it turned out so well," Slickenside said, jumping into the breach. "Some of my best friends are Sedimentaries, but really, they're happier in their own neighborhoods.   Why, I remember..."

"Ooh, Ouoch, Sorry! The way my hip hurts," said Big Blue, "I need to lie down for awhile. Why don't you two youngsters check out those Sedimentaries and come back later. I'll feel like entertaining again after my nap."

THE BIG ONE!

Dusty MacBugTussle was sitting on the big blue boulder behind his cabin one forenoon, contemplating the state of the fishing, which was poor. "Vegetable, mineral, animal," he said. "Mineral, animal, vegetable." "Whatever are you doing, dear?" asked Madge MacBugTussle, coming out of the cabin. "Our little daughter and I were playing a guessing game, dear. And I was just thinking that the trout I catch are animals, but fossilized fish are minerals." "Interesting point, dear, but not too practical, I fear. Lunch in an hour, dear." She went back into the cabin humming "animal, vegetable, mineral" and smiling tenderly.

No sooner had she left than who came walking up from the lake but Dusty's old friend, Professor J.W. Slickenside, of the Department of Geology at the Great Public University. Clearly he was dressed for field work, with khaki shirt and trousers, field boots, and a Sherlock Holmes billed hat. He carried a rock hammer.

"Well, hi, John Wesley," Dusty said, for the two were on a first name—also on a second name—basis, "Congratulations on your promotion to Piltdown Professor of Paleontology in charge of all fossils, both living and dead at the G.P.U., a very important position."

"Thanks, Dusty."

"What's this I hear about that animal/mineral disappearing from the G.P.U.?"

"That's what I'm here for. One of our Brontosaurs has disappeared. Unfortunately, she was in my department, and I'm rather in hot water till we get her back. The President of the G.P.U. said to spare no expense; the reputation of the university is at stake."

"Did you say Brontosaur?" Dusty asked. "Afraid I'm not acquainted with that kind of fish. What's she look like?"

"Well, she's about seventy feet long, with a big body and a small head and tail—not very brainy. In fact, we're surprised she even could find her way out of the basement of the Earth Science building where she lived."

"Seventy feet! Magnificent! Why the biggest trout I've ever caught was just a shade over thirty six inches, even after a little stretching for the sake of the story. A seventy-foot fish would set a freshwater angling record that wouldn't be beaten for years perhaps never."

"I was hoping you'd like to help hunt her," Slickenside said. "You have a solid reputation for unbelievable catches. I know your alma mater, the G.P.U., will reward you well for finding her. In fact, they might even award you an honorary Doctorate of Piscatology."

MacBugTussle threw his hat in the air. "Wow! Wait till I get my gear. What shall we use for bait?"

"She must be very hungry. She was just skin and bones—in fact mostly bones—when she disappeared. She's a vegetarian; perhaps a cabbage or even a nice cantaloupe would attract her."

MacBugTussle clapped his hat back on as he ran to his cabin. He soon emerged carrying a pole with the circumference of a baseball bat and twice as long as he was tall. Attached to the top was a big pulley and ratchet affair with a hook on the end of a stout woven steel cable.

"Where'd you get that?" Slickenside asked, casting a dubious eye on the fishing equipment.

"I just happened to have it around," MacBugTussle replied. "It's my come-along winch rigged on a piece of pole I got to put up my wife's new curtains. Don't worry! I'll replace it before she even knows it's gone."

It took both his hands to carry the gear, but under his arm he held a two-pound chunk of cheddar cheese. "I can't imagine a fish eating cabbage or cantaloupe," he explained. "But the vegetarians of my acquaintance all eat cheese, and so do trout. We'll try it."

"What about a landing net?" Slickenside inquired.

"No," MacBugTussle decided. "There isn't room in the boat. We'll just play her till she's tired and work her around till we can slide her out on the shore."

But, as on many another fishing expedition, action was slow. The two anglers who set out so hopefully returned at lunch time without even as much as a nibble.

"The light is wrong," MacBugTussle said. "We'll try again this evening."

"Maybe we'd better fish in the big lake this time," Slickenside suggested when they set out after dinner. "The small lake hardly leaves space for a seventy foot long animal to turn around."

Hardly had they dropped the bait over than there was a hearty tug, and a huge snout broke the surface. It moved right on up swallowing cheese, hook, winch, and pole. In a second bite, the monster took boat, motor, and anglers. Fortunately for MacBugTussle and Slickenside, it merely swished them around in its mouth and sneezed them out again, "which goes to prove," Slickenside observed jubilantly, "that Brontosaurs really are vegetarians."

MacBugTussle, whose pants were torn from ankle to hip in the encounter, was only slightly less elated. "Don't let go of the boat painter," he admonished Slickenside. "We're onto a big one now."

The monster had a different idea. She spit out the painter, fastened the men with an evil reptilian stare, and hissed with a blast like a bursting firehose. The force of air caught the two as they swam, lifted them like feathers off the surface of the water and deposited them far up the shore.

The two fishermen took stock as they got to their feet. Slickenside's neat khaki shirt and trousers were muddy and torn, the visor of his cap was askew. He'd lost his rock hammer and one of his boots. With every step he took, water squished out of a hole in the other.

MacBugTussle's costume was slightly less disheveled, but a large smear of black grease across his face made him a like companion to his friend. In fact the two of them could have doubled as desperadoes in a third rate western movie.

By the time they could get themselves sorted out, the monster, boat, and gear had disappeared. They had only a trailing bit of painter and their appearances to corroborate their tale.

"Never mind," MacBugTussle said, as they walked around the lake toward a group of fishermen. "We'll get some bigger gear and return. Let's tell these folks and ask them to help."

"Right," Slickenside agreed. "Hi, people, we've just lost a monster fish, and we need help to recapture it." He smiled crookedly and lurched toward them with his one bare and one booted foot, holding out the rope in one hand and his torn cap in the other.

To their surprise, the men dropped their fishing equipment, scrambled to their feet, and scattered, shouting "Madmen! Run for your life!"

"Maybe we better just keep quiet till we catch her again," Slickenside suggested as the two climbed up to the trail and made their way to the end of the lake.

MacBugTussle agreed, "Peculiar people," he observed. "They'll be sorry. They're missing the chance of a lifetime to catch a really big trophy fish."

The young man at the dock twitched his eyebrows with surprise when they got to the resort. But all he said was, "Telegram for you Dr. Slickenside."

"I'll get it while you pick up a newspaper," John

Wesley suggested to Dusty. "Meet you at the soda fountain."

"Well, by golly," he said as MacBugTussle handed him a chocolate milkshake. "The wire is from the Great Public University, 'Brontosaur has returned. All is forgiven. Please come home!'"

"Hunh," said MacBugTussle, "look at this." He laid the paper on the counter.

"Loch Ness Monster disappears. Believed to be vacationing in Lake Tahoe area."

"We'd a gotten a big one if we'd just had a way to land it. I'm sorry I didn't take your suggestion of the net."

Just then Madge MacBugTussle came out of the cabin and walked over toward the big blue boulder where Dusty sat. "Wake up, dear; lunch is ready. Be sure to wash your hands and face."

ALSO FROM
TALKING MOUNTAIN PUBLISHING:

If you enjoyed this book, you might like *Sierra Summers: Fireside Tales to Share with Young and Old*, also by Margaret Trussell. It is a collection of two dozen good humored, upbeat tales, some true and some fiction, drawn from the author's experiences over more than fifty years.

The setting for most of them is a mountain lake in California near Lake Tahoe. The stories convey a strong sense of place, sensitively depicting the landscape, the people, and the plants and animals of this rugged land.

To order one or both books send $10.95 each plus shipping and handling (we pay the tax).

Order form is on the next page.

BOOK ORDER

Number of copies of *Sierra Summers*_____

Number of *North of the Golden Gate*_____

Total number of books ordered_____

Total cost of books @ $10.95 each_____

Shipping one or more copies to
same address ($2.50)   Shipping_____

PLEASE ENCLOSE CHECK OR MONEY ORDER (Sorry, no
credit cards.)

I ENCLOSE $_____

Send to_____

Address_____

City/State_____ Zip_____

If you would like the books autographed, please
check here___ and state for whom:

_____

If above is a gift please fill in below:

My Name_____

Address_____

City/State_____ Zip_____

Talking Mountain Publishing Co.
PO Box B-621
Bodega Bay, California 94923-0621